TWILIGHT'S PROMISE

❧❧❧❧

AN AGENTS OF HIS NOVEL

❧❧❧❧

SHEILA KELL

Editing and Formatting: Lea Schizas
Photographer: Paul Henry Serres Photography
Model: Tommy Villeneuve

ISBN (Print): 978-1-957587-22-6
ISBN (E-Book): 978-1-957587-21-9

Printed in the USA

Titles by Sheila Kell

<u>HIS SERIES</u>

His Desire

His Choice

His Return

His Chance

His Destiny

His Family

His Heart

His Fantasy

A Hamilton Christmas

<u>AGENTS OF HIS SERIES</u>

Evening Shadows

Midnight Escape

Afternoon Delight

Bayou Sunset

Chasing Shadows at Dusk

Moonlight Exception

When Daylight Breaks

Twilight's Promise

<u>COASTAL INVESTIGATION SERIES</u>

Deadly Betrayal

Read Between the Lines

Fractured Trust

To Lea Schizas
You've served as my editor, formatter,
cover designer, and advisor throughout the years.
I can't picture writing a book without you.

CHAPTER ONE

If she hadn't forgotten her credit card at the store, they might've walked right into the thief who broke into her apartment.

Ava Sinclair's heart thundered in her chest, each beat amplifying her mounting nerves. Her gaze darted around the room as disbelief sank in. Someone had broken in and stolen her prized, expensive laptop. Everything else was untouched. Her cash, jewelry, and even personal mementos were all left pristine. Only her computer was gone, replaced by a chilling note: "You're next." Goosebumps prickled on her arms as a shiver raced down her spine.

"We need to call the police." Emily Hamilton, her lifelong friend, re-entered the living room after searching every corner for clues.

Ava snorted bitterly, a cocktail of skepticism and frustration swirling within her. "What's the point? Will they dust for prints and solve this before the city's crime and murder rates climb even higher?"

Emily's face hardened. "They might not crack the case overnight, but if the evidence turns up, maybe—just maybe—you'll get your computer back. Doing nothing isn't an option. Besides, this note unsettles me."

Ava hesitated, caught in a swirl of fear and hope. Yet, law enforcement had dismissed her warnings about the encrypted note she uncovered during the latest financial data breach, leaving her feeling overlooked.

Could this threatening message be related?

As a cybersecurity expert, she was hired to track down and trace breaches from compromised data. When the bank called, she sprang into action. While she hadn't pinpointed the source of the breach, she was certain of one thing—that encrypted message hidden within held the secrets someone needed to uncover.

Despite her efforts to explain, the Federal Trade Commission and the FBI dismissed her entirely. They seemed annoyed, perceiving her attempts to trace the breach as overstepping, even though it was their official domain to investigate. The frustration of being ignored by the very agencies meant to protect her had her scoffing at even local law enforcement.

With Emily as a forensic accountant, Ava had initially planned to explain the mysterious encrypted message to her. But now, with the added note, she decided it was safer to keep it under wraps for the moment. Her mind raced, trying to decipher whether the note truly signaled danger or was just a sick joke. Was she next? Or was it something else entirely? She couldn't even finish the thought—it sounded too absurd. After all, her computer had been stolen, plain and simple.

Knowing her friend wouldn't let up, she finally relented. "Okay, I'll call the police." She fished her phone out of her purse, which she had set down near the pile of books they'd bought that day. As she dialed the non-emergency number, Emily reached into the refrigerator and grabbed two cans of soda.

While they waited for the officer to arrive, the two women turned their attention to the day's haul. The local independent bookstore's sidewalk sale had been irresistible, and as book lovers, they couldn't resist diving into their new treasures.

They started their day over a cozy brunch, laughter bubbling between them as they planned their day. Afterward, they wandered into the bookstore, their conversation lively and animated, catching up on Emily's two mischievous children, whose antics had them both giggling. Ava couldn't help but wonder if she'd ever experience parenthood herself.

"I've never tried a Blind Date with a Book experience." Emily held up the wrapped novel, which looked like it was bursting with surprises and goodies spilling from its pages.

"Me neither." Ava smiled. "But it sounded like fun."

They eagerly unpacked the contents in the beautifully wrapped book's covering: an eye mask, a comforting cup of tea, a review card, two bookmarks, a pen, and a highlighter with tabs for annotations. Definitely a treasure trove for any book lover.

Ava's eyes sparkled, and she waved to Emily. "Go ahead, open yours first. I want to see what's inside."

Emily giggled like a child on Christmas morning. She tore into the wrapping and gasped, her face lighting up with delight. Ava knew instantly that it was one of Emily's favorite authors, and a book she'd wanted to purchase but had returned to the shelf.

"Your turn."

Ava's heart fluttered with anticipation, hoping her luck would be as fortunate as Emily's, who always seemed to pick the perfect reads. As she eagerly tore into the flowered kraft paper wrapping, her brows furrowed in curiosity. The book was unfamiliar. She didn't recognize the author or title. Turning it over, she scanned the back cover, then finally opened it. Excitement surged through her when she saw the signature. "Look, it's signed by the author."

"Oh, wow." Emily pointed to the vivid cover. "I love that cover."

Discreet covers were all the rage now, and Ava had been curious but hadn't yet jumped on the bandwagon. But this one called to her, making her eager to start a collection of beautifully hidden treasures.

Finally setting their books aside, Ava and Emily settled into a relaxed chat while waiting for the authorities to arrive. Ava knew it would be hours before anyone showed up, and though she didn't want to keep Emily, she enjoyed the unexpected company. Since leaving the government to work independently, Ava had watched her old coworkers gradually drift away, leaving her to run her small operation alone. Any interaction, therefore, was a welcome distraction.

Emily set her soda can down with a click. "What have you been working on lately?"

Ava hesitated, pondering whether to confide in Emily about the mysterious coded message. The note had felt like just a fluke—hadn't it?

"A bank suffered a data breach recently. They've got

me trying to trace it down."

Emily's eyes shone bright with interest. "That sounds fascinating. How's it going?"

Scoffing playfully, Ava set her drink on the coffee table. "Nowhere. Just getting started." She smiled mischievously. "But I'll crack it."

Emily chuckled, her face lighting up with genuine warmth. "That's my girl. I can't believe the FTC hasn't come down on you yet for doing what they're supposed to do."

Ava shook her head, frustration flickering in her eyes. "They're so lazy. You know I—"

"Hate lazy people," Emily finished promptly, a teasing smile playing on her lips.

They both burst into giggles, their camaraderie shining through.

Ava grinned. "You know me so well."

When a sudden knock echoed through the quiet, Ava's heart leapt into her throat, her pulse quickening with a surge of fear. Almost immediately, she shook her head, trying to dismiss the irrational worry. It was only the police. Thieves didn't knock before breaking in, after all. With hesitant steps, she rose and approached the door, casting a wary glance into the peephole to confirm it was a uniformed officer standing outside.

She opened the door. "Thank you for coming." She wanted to avoid any potential awkwardness before it could arise.

But the female officer just pulled out a small notepad, her tone sharp and no-nonsense. "I hear you had a break-in."

Ava felt a flicker of irritation flare up. She didn't need

more tense interactions with law enforcement on what was already a rough day.

Had she already contacted the authorities this morning, before she and Emily set out on their little adventure? It all felt like a distant memory now.

"Yes. Someone stole my computer."

"May I come in?" The officer's eyes didn't meet Ava's. Instead, they scanned the apartment.

Ava hesitated for a moment before stepping aside. "Of course."

As the officer brushed past her, the woman suddenly froze, eyes bright with recognition. "Emily?"

Emily's face lit up in a gasp, and she sprang to her feet. "Evelyn. It's so good to see you."

The tension in the room dissolved instantly, replaced by lingering smiles.

Ava quickly closed the door, turning sharply. She raised an eyebrow. "I take it you two know each other?"

Emily stood and grinned warmly. "We went to high school together. Evelyn and I were in the Math Club."

Evelyn nodded, a playful smirk on her lips. "But Emily was definitely the real brains of the team."

Emily blushed. "No, it was a team effort."

Evelyn chuckled. Then, turning to Ava, she said, "Now, about that break-in."

Ava hesitated. "It's not just any computer. It's used for cybersecurity."

Evelyn's brow furrowed in confusion.

"Never mind." Ava quickly handed her a slip of paper she'd grabbed from her desk. "Here's the serial number."

Evelyn studied it, her expression serious. "Great. That'll be helpful if we manage to recover it."

Ava shot a pointed look at Emily, as if to say, "See? They're not going to do a thing."

Evelyn carefully copied the serial number into her notebook, her tone professional. "Anything else taken?"

Ava shook her head, her voice matter-of-fact. "No. Just the computer." Her work computer. She had urgent projects pending. At least her data was stored on a cloud server.

She'd have to order a new computer overnight.

"What time did this happen?"

Ava answered each question efficiently. "The lock wasn't broken…Yes, the building has cameras, but none in my apartment…No, I have no idea who stole the computer." She hesitated before refusing to show the note left behind. What difference would it make? Nothing. Just like Evelyn, standing there, doing nothing.

Evelyn nodded, heading for the door. "If you hear anything, let us know."

Ava closed the door, exhaling slowly. She turned to Emily, who had returned to the couch. "That was a big waste of time."

Emily's smile was warm but optimistic. "You never know. Maybe they'll recover it. The building has cameras, after all."

Ava scoffed, sarcasm tipping her tone. "Like they'll ask for those. This is a nothing case for them, just a side note."

"Speaking of notes, why didn't you show Evelyn the one that the thief left?" Emily's question hung in the air, her curiosity sparking.

Ava sank onto the couch. "Because they wouldn't have done anything."

But Emily wasn't convinced. "I'd like to show it to Devon and Jesse." The names carried weight. They were her older brothers and the experienced duo behind Hamilton Investigation and Security. An elite firm that did jobs even Ava didn't know about.

"What could they do?"

"They'd actually check for prints. That might lead us to who took your computer and threatened you." With unwavering conviction in her voice, Emily's eyes sparkled.

The idea of catching the culprit sounded promising enough to convince Ava. "Take the note. Let's see if we can catch this guy since the police won't."

A smile tugged at Emily's lips. "Thank you. By the way, about your computer—do you think you can get another one quickly?"

Ava nodded confidently. "Yeah, overnight. But I'll have to download a ton of software to make it work for my projects."

Emily chuckled. "You were always busy, even when you worked for the government. Juggling side projects kept you on your toes."

Ava glanced away, a flicker of discomfort crossing her face. She didn't want to admit that her relentless schedule was more about avoiding silence. It was about avoiding the loneliness that crept in when she wasn't busy. At thirty-two, the ticking biological clock felt deafening. It was time to decide whether she'd have children or accept a life without them.

Emily waved her hand in front of Ava's face. "Where'd you go just now?"

Ava shook her head, forcing a smile. "Nowhere. Just

thinking about everything I need to catch up on." But truthfully, her mind was elsewhere. She conjured the reasons she kept herself frantic and busy. Her life had been a whirlwind ever since she'd been stood up at the altar, and she wasn't sure if the tight hold she kept on life was healing or just hiding the ache inside.

Emily rose to her feet, and Ava followed suit. "It's about time I head home. AJ can only juggle Alex and Pamela for so long."

Her own biological clock echoed again. Tick. Tick. Tick. Instead of the usual grumbling or sarcasm, she grinned warmly. "I bet he loves every second of it."

With a gentle, affectionate smile, Emily grabbed her shopping bag. "He does. But those little troublemakers sure keep him on his toes."

Ava chuckled, imagining the formidable Hamilton brother racing after energetic children. "At least they're out of diapers now."

Emily shuddered. "I never left him alone with them back then. Once, he got sick after one of them made a mess." She shook her head. "Poor guy."

Ava giggled, about to speak—

Suddenly, a thunderous knock shattered the moment. Ava spun around, ready for trouble. Or perhaps the police had returned.

But instead, a loud, commanding voice boomed from outside. "FBI, open up!"

Emily's eyes widened. "What did you do?"

CHAPTER TWO

Rob "Grits" Grimes returned from burying his father—a man he quietly despised—to find his team on an op. With no real reason to join, he felt compelled by a restless need to do something, anything, to channel the storm of anger inside him. The man he'd reluctantly called "Dad" had been an alcoholic, and those weekly phone calls to "check in on his son" always masked his true intent of borrowing money he never paid back.

Grits experienced a lot of hardship during his childhood. His father was a relentless drunk, drifting from one failed job to another, and often losing control enough to beat his wife and children. Growing up, Grits became his younger brother and sister's protector, stepping into the line of fire and taking their beatings to shield them. As the years passed and his father's rage grew more unpredictable, Grits found himself powerless to stop the violence.

When his father finally died, Grits felt a strange sense of relief—guilt flickered there, but it was faint, overshadowed by a profound sense of freedom.

At HIS headquarters, in the war room, Grits watched

Devon work diligently at his computer. A former CIA agent and a wizard with technology, Devon's skills were nothing short of incredible. He could find almost anything online, and today, his focus was razor-sharp as he unraveled some digital mystery.

Jesse crept up behind him and gave his shoulder a firm slap. "New tattoos?"

Grits' eyes flicked downward to his chest, where a bold skull tattoo commemorated his father's passing, its dark lines stark against his skin. His gaze shifted to his arm, tracing the intricately woven design that snaked down to the back of his hand—a haunting reminder of his mother's loss, etched into his skin and soul. He nodded, knowing Jesse didn't need the details. The answer was visible. "Yeah."

Jesse's eyes softened, studying him like he could read his soul. "How are your brother and sister?"

Both relieved to be free from Dad's chaos. "They're good."

Jesse paused, as if he saw through the mask. Then he nodded quietly. "Listen, I'm sorry you missed the team. With both squads out, there's not much for you to do right now."

He was the team leader of Bravo, responsible for the mission's success. I should've gone with them. But he'd chosen differently. He'd stayed for his father's funeral, for the family…what remained of it.

At this point, he'd gladly take anything to keep busy. "Do you have any investigative tasks I can help with?" Since the brothers had stepped away from the field into their family's investigative side, the teams worked closely with them during operations.

Jesse shook his head. "Nothing right now. We've got it all under control."

Of course, they did. Running their operation like a well-oiled machine, the brothers were in high demand—not just for field missions but also for occasional covert assignments with the government.

Before Grits could say another word, Jesse's phone buzzed loudly.

His face softened into a smile as he saw the caller ID. "It's Em. Let me take this."

Grits nodded, watching Jesse step aside to talk with his sister. It took him back to that last moment he saw his sister after the funeral, before she and her husband left for New Mexico, where he was stationed at a military base. His sister had always claimed she'd never marry someone in the military, yet here she was—married to a civilian contractor working with the military. Truly, life's ironies never cease to surprise.

To keep from wandering into the shadows of his depressing memories, he approached Devon with a casual smile. "How's it going?"

Devon looked up from his computer, a grin spreading across his face. "Great. Mitch and Theresa are growing like weeds. They keep Rylee and me on our toes."

The Hamilton family had all met their wives during operations. That shared history had woven itself into the teams, and one by one, he'd watched the men step into the sacred vows of marriage. The thought made him shudder. No, he wouldn't marry someone from an operation. When he did marry—if he ever did—it'd be on his terms.

Somehow.

Smiling at the mental image of Devon and Rylee chasing after their young kids, Grits nodded in agreement. "I can see that."

Devon leaned in slightly, sincerity in his eyes. "Hey, I'm sorry you missed your team."

He nodded, a bit wistful. "So am I. You're sure I can't join them?"

Devon shook his head. "Not this time. They've gone dark for the next twenty-four hours. Should be back soon."

They would be successful. They were always successful. Not always pretty, but successful.

He nodded his understanding. "What's happening with Stone?"

Joe Stone once thrived as an agent within the team, but he decided to shift focus to the computer side of operations. Having two hands at the keyboard was useful, yet Stone struggled to keep up at first, relying heavily on Devon's expertise.

Devon nodded. "He's improving every day," he said, a hint of pride in his tone. "One day, he'll be ready to take over for me."

Grits scoffed, a grin curling his lips. "Yeah, right. Like you'd ever hand over full control of this baby." He shot a glance at Devon's supercomputer and the three blinking monitors.

Devon chuckled, unmistakable in his confidence. "You know me too well."

Jesse approached, phone pressed to his ear. "We'll handle it." With the call ended, he turned to Grits.

"Excuse me, Grits, I need to speak with my brothers."

Grits' ears perked up. Could this be an operation where he could actually contribute? But then he hesitated. What kind of operation could he run solo? None. It had to be an investigation. That was probably the reason why the family gathered at headquarters: to discuss business. Sure, they shared laughs and personal stories, but Jesse's stern expression kept things serious.

Grits headed to the locker room, opened his locker, and grabbed his tennis shoes and a fresh set of shorts to go with his T-shirt. After changing out of his cargo pants and boots, he headed to the workout room, fueling a desire to burn off the ghosts of his fucked-up childhood.

He grabbed two dumbbells and began doing curls, feeling the strain in his biceps as he lifted a weight heavier than usual. The burn seared into his muscles, but he pushed through, lost in thought.

Memories flooded his mind. He'd missed Pup and Elena's unexpected wedding with the joy and the camaraderie. But that happiness was bitter now, overshadowed by grief. His younger brother's voice had trembled when he informed Grits of the death and asked for help with the funeral costs. Without hesitation, he agreed. He always did. He paid for everything, carrying the weight of guilt and loss for his family. They'd endured so much with emotional scars and physical pain, and he was determined to take their burdens.

Before he could sink deeper into his grief, the man he'd mentioned earlier strolled into the workout room, momentarily shifting the mood. Grits nodded in recognition. "Hey, Stone."

Stone nodded back and moved to a barbell, silently adding weights with practiced ease.

They'd been working out for about five minutes when Grits finally broke the silence. "How are the kids?"

Stone, who had come to HIS married, responded with quiet pride. His wife had left him, but he shared joint custody of the children. "They're good. My weekend's coming up, and we're planning a trip to the zoo. The kids love it there."

Grits shifted the conversation. "And how's the computer side of things holding up?"

Stone grunted as he lifted the loaded bar above his head, then set it down smoothly. "That's going well. Devon's a real computer wizard. Honestly, I don't think I'll ever catch up to him."

Hearing the door open, Grits turned. Daylan from the elusive Charlie team was standing there, a confident smile on his face.

"Mind if I join you?" He stepped inside without waiting for an answer.

"Go right ahead," Grits muttered, sarcasm lacing his words, but his remark went unnoticed. He recalled meeting the K9 handler when Pup had risked everything to save Elena. He'd come to help, even though Pup hadn't wanted his assistance. That was ancient history now.

Stone cleared his throat, softening his tone. "Sorry about your dad, Grits."

Grits nodded quietly. "Thanks." His childhood wounds were his own, and the passing of his father didn't shake him. He wasn't about to let them see how much the memories hurt.

Daylan stepped onto the treadmill, punching in his desired speed and elevation. "Oh man." He shook his head. "That really sucks."

Grits nodded politely and said, "Thanks," a gesture that was more habit than surprise. He cleared his throat, shifting the mood. "So, how's Charlie team coming along?"

They'd been formed years ago, yet they still operated on the fringes of the other units. They'd met briefly, but never truly integrated. Charlie team handled the covert missions the government couldn't—or wouldn't—touch.

"Things are good. We're about to disperse for a couple of weeks since we're in for a bit of a standstill."

Yet, Daylan was here instead of heading home or visiting loved ones. Maybe he had no one waiting.

Before the conversation could pick up, Jesse appeared in the gym. "Grits, can you come here for a minute?"

"Sure." Grits set the dumbbells back in their rack, exchanged quick farewell glances with the two men, and moved to follow Jesse.

As he stepped out, his eyes caught Daylan's intense stare. He felt slightly unnerved, as if being watched by a hawk.

Following Jesse, he retraced his steps toward the war room, anticipation building. When they stopped, Jesse's serious expression caught him off guard. He sensed this wasn't good news.

Then, Jesse casually dropped the bombshell. "I've got a job for you."

A surge of adrenaline hit Grits, barely containing his excitement beneath a calm exterior. "Okay." He made sure to mask the thrill rushing through him.

"It's a babysitting detail."

Grits shrugged, relaxing a bit—anything was better than a routine day. "What's the full story?"

"That's the thing. There's not much to go on."

Intrigued, Grits raised an eyebrow. "Go on."

Jesse shook his head briefly and then continued. "It's Emily's best friend. Her computer was stolen."

Grits' brow furrowed. He couldn't believe what he was hearing. Going into protection detail over a stolen computer?

Jesse's face sharpened. "And the thief left a note."

Grits' interest piqued. "What did it say?"

Then Jesse dropped the second bombshell. "You're next."

Holy fuck. "Who's doing the detail with me?" He scanned the quiet room. With the teams out, it had to be a Hamilton brother because everyone else was busy.

For the first time since he'd been at HIS, Jesse looked uneasy. "It's only you."

His eyebrows shot up. What? Could he really handle protective duty alone? Unless he was prepared to live with the woman, which didn't sound appealing at all. He took a deep breath, feeling the weight of the task ahead, knowing this wasn't going to be as simple as it seemed.

Jesse cleared his throat, a hint of skepticism in his voice. "Yeah, she doesn't want a security detail."

He arched a brow. "So, why are we even offering it?"

"Because Emily insisted—and convinced her that one of us should stay with her."

"Stay with her?" The words sent a chill down his

spine. He knew that was the logical move, but hearing it out loud made his stomach tighten. Nothing good ever came from a situation like that. They'd either clash fiercely or end up in bed together. The space in between was nonexistent.

"Yeah. She's got an extra room and is willing to let someone stay, as long as—and I quote—'They don't get in my way.'"

That's just perfect. One of those types. The fiercely independent ones, convinced they can handle everything on their own. Who knew? Maybe she really could. But still, why bother offering help at all?

"Listen. I know it's a crappy detail, but it's all I've got for you."

And, he needed something. Maybe, just maybe, he could find that elusive middle ground in living with an unknown woman for an indefinite period. "How long?"

Jesse shrugged. "Until we can figure out who sent the note."

With Devon's mad skills, that shouldn't take long—a few days at most.

"Okay. I'm in."

CHAPTER THREE

Ava couldn't believe she was actually considering letting a complete stranger stay in her apartment. Emily, as usual, was overreacting. She had blown the situation out of proportion, especially about the threatening note. Here Ava was, frantically cleaning her spare room, transforming it into a cozy haven for a man she'd never even met.

After the FBI had come and gone, it took some quick thinking to calm Emily down. The agents weren't interested in the encrypted message she'd uncovered during her investigation. They just didn't want her poking around the breach. Heck, they blew off the threatening note. To them, the interview was routine, and honestly, they seemed annoyed about the whole thing.

But she knew better. She decided to decrypt the message herself. Her skills were enough for that. As she bit her thumbnail—a nervous habit from her teens—she realized her backup laptop just wouldn't cut it. It was clunky, old, and meant only for emergencies. Well, this was an emergency and then some. All she needed was to place her order, and she'd have a brand-new laptop in no time, ready to crack the code.

It could be nothing more than a message planted by those who caused the breach—a suspicion she clung to, yet part of her wondered if there was more to it. The adrenaline kicked in, her heart pounding as she imagined the possibilities. Maybe someone was selling stolen data before it was even compromised. Or perhaps they were secretly funneling information to another country. The thought sent a shiver down her spine. Regardless, this was a mystery she had to unravel. Leaving no stone unturned, she refused to let an encrypted message hidden within a breach go unnoticed.

She scanned the guest room, giving a nod of approval. It would do. Next, she checked the apartment's only bathroom and made sure it was spotless. Frustration bubbled inside her. Cleaning for a stranger she didn't even want in her space felt like a chore she shouldn't have to do. Sure, the apartment could always benefit from a deep clean, but she'd only recently finished one.

With the room deemed acceptable, she moved to the living room, silently praying he wouldn't peek into her room. It wasn't the tidiest corner of her place, but it was a balance—neither messy nor pristine, just her comfort zone.

Her phone rang, slicing through the quiet of the room. Ava searched until she found it on her desk. With a quick swipe, she answered, voice steady but tinged with firm resolve. "Hi, Em. I've changed my mind. No one needs to stay with me. It was just a note left by some petty thief."

"Oh no," Emily's voice crackled through. "You're not

backing out of this. It wasn't just a petty thief. It was a damn good one. They broke into your apartment without leaving a trace."

Ava grimaced, recalling the scene. Fingerprints, maybe, but no police or FBI investigation—just the usual shrug. They'd decided it was a petty thief eyeing her laptop in town and figuring it was an easy score.

Before Ava could protest, Emily pressed on. "Grits is on his way. You'll like him. He's nice, polite—"

A snort escaped Ava. "Nice and polite" usually meant they weren't exactly eye candy, which didn't bother her. She wasn't planning to look to him for companionship. No, she wondered, what was she expecting from him? Protection? From what exactly? This whole thing had spiraled out of control, and she was more than ready to put an end to it.

"I don't need protection." Her voice was firm, signaling she was done with the drama.

Emily sighed deeply. "Just humor me for a bit, okay? I'm genuinely worried about you."

Humoring her shouldn't mean inviting some impeccably nice, overly polite stranger into her personal space. "I don't know, Em."

"Please, just give it a few days. Devon's going to work on the code—and yes, I'm still super annoyed you didn't tell me about this right away—then you'll be free from Grits' protection."

A few days. She chewed her thumbnail, then quickly caught herself. What's a few days if the note might actually be a real threat? She'd be busy anyway. He could just watch TV until she or Em's brother managed to decrypt the message.

She hated the idea of someone else helping her crack the encryption. She wanted to be the one to investigate, to dive into the code herself.

But in the end, she nodded, realizing it was better to play it safe. "Okay, but just for two days. That's it. No extensions."

A sudden knock echoed on the door, causing her to frown in irritation. Grits—what a ridiculous name—was already there. Em hadn't been taking no for an answer, not that she ever did.

"Looks like he's here. I've got to go. Talk to you later." She swiftly ended the call before Em could even respond. She then moved to the door, heart pounding with a mix of annoyance and curiosity. Peering through the peephole, she saw a well-dressed man who appeared reasonably handsome. Not that she was complaining. He was definitely better than the usual "nice and polite" types that she dreaded.

For a moment, she chuckled inwardly at her own thoughts, wondering why she was already feeling nervous about this stranger.

Putting on her best smile, she opened the door. "Hi. You must be Grits—"

A voice boomed down the hallway, commanding, "Ava," as the man she couldn't see drew closer. "Close that door!" When she stayed frozen, he lashed out with a sharp yell, "Now!"

Anxiety tightened her chest as the venom in his voice cut through the silence. Her eyes locked on the figure in front of her—the sneer on his face, the large knife clenched in his grip—sending an icy shiver down her spine. Heart pounding, she hurriedly slammed the door shut as he swung out with the knife, locked it, and darted toward her desk where her phone lay.

Trembling fingers clutched the device as she fumbled to dial 911, uncertainty prickling her mind about what help they could truly offer. Suddenly, loud shouts echoed through the hallway, followed by a fierce scuffle, just as the line connected.

"Nine-one-one, what's your emergency?" The dispatcher's calm voice broke through the chaos, anchoring her in this terrifying moment.

"There's a man with a knife—"

A sudden rush of fear tightened her chest. The words were barely out of her mouth before a calm voice called out to her. "Ava, it's Grits. You can open the door now. It's safe."

But Ava's head shook fiercely. No, it wasn't safe. Her eyes flicked to the door, where a man with a glinting knife had loomed, threatening and unpredictable.

"Ma'am?" the 911 dispatcher prompted softly, waiting. But Ava's breath hitched, paralyzed by the threat just beyond the door.

Urgent pounding echoed against her door. "Ava, hurry up!"

Her heart raced as she hesitated, uncertain whether to trust her instincts or the chaos outside. She disconnected the 911 call and slowly approached the door. "How can I be sure it's really you?"

"Call Em and have her describe me, but hurry the fuck up. This guy might have friends."

Her fingers slid over her quick dial, her pulse racing. When Em answered, she nearly shouted, "There's a man with a knife out here, and now this guy claims he's Grits, but I can't tell. I don't want to open the door."

"Calm down, Ava. Hold tight. Let me call Grits. Stay right there."

Ava drew a few trembling breaths, her mind a whirlwind of panic over a man wielding a knife and another shouting at her. In Baltimore, such chaos was common—except, not for her.

Suddenly, a phone rang outside her door, and a man's voice commanded, "Em, get her to open this damn door." Moments of tense silence followed before he added, "Uh-huh. Okay, I'll try."

Ava's stomach churned at the word "try," and she glanced around desperately for a weapon, just in case he forced his way in.

Then, the voice outside cleared its throat. "Em says to tell you that you kissed some guy named Warren under the bleachers at a football game and that you never told because he claimed you were a bad kisser."

Her breath hitched in shock. How dare Em broadcast that embarrassing secret to a stranger? Steeling herself, she unlocked the door.

Before she could open it, it abruptly swung open, and the man stormed in, urgency etched on his face. "Hurry, we don't have time to play around." His eyes darted around as if expecting trouble behind every shadow.

Ava silently closed the door behind him, her eyes narrowing as she took in the man who had just breezed into her space under the so-called guise of "protecting her." He was strikingly handsome with a fierce edge that sent a shiver down her spine. No wonder the guy with the knife had backed off.

When she didn't reply, he broke the silence, his voice firm yet tense. "Grab a bag. We can't stay here."

Ava's brow furrowed as she glanced around her apartment, confusion flickering. "Why not?" She was proud of herself for her voice remaining steady despite her racing thoughts.

His eyes locked onto hers. "Because it'd be easy to take you out."

Ava scoffed, crossing her arms defiantly. "No one's taking me out." But then, she recalled the guy with the knife. Her voice quivered slightly. "Okay, so someone might come at me, but…you'll be here to protect me, right?"

He looked down at her from his towering six-foot-something frame, eyes firm. "We're going to the safe house. That's not negotiable."

Her stomach clenched at the thought—leaving, going somewhere alone with this stranger, who no one knew where they were. No way, no how. "I'm not going anywhere with you."

His gaze darkened. "Woman, if I have to toss you over my shoulder, you're coming. Now, grab your bag. We're wasting time."

When she still didn't move, he let out a heavy sigh. "Hell, this was supposed to be an easy gig." He reached into his pants pocket, pulled out his phone with a quick flick, and speed-dialed a number. "Em, talk some sense into your friend. And we don't have all day. I've already dispatched one gang member. There are going to be more."

A shiver coursed down her spine at his words. More? After her? What on earth was happening? What had she done to trigger this mess? It'd only been a break-in and a theft of her computer.

He handed her the phone with a steady grip. "Here."

She reached out cautiously, taking the device from him, feeling a jolt from the brief contact. "Em? What's he rambling on about?"

"Sorry, Ava. You have to do exactly what he says. He knows how to handle trouble."

Ava hesitated, thinking he was trouble himself, but she kept her thoughts to herself. "He wants to go to a safe house, but I don't want to hide away. I need a new computer. I have work to do."

But Em cut her off gently. "You can do both from the safe house. Grits has a phone and a credit card ready for you to use. So you can get your new computer and keep up with everything."

Her eyebrows shot up. A phone and a credit card? They'd planned this out more thoroughly than she'd realized. What happened to just watching out for a thief?

"Ava," Em continued, "you need to do this. I know it sounds strange and surreal, but you're really in danger."

Who really posed the threat? Was it a lurking thief ready to strike, or the man standing directly in front of her, whose intentions she couldn't quite read? The next moment could change everything.

"Okay, I'll go. But only for a few days."

CHAPTER FOUR

It took every ounce of Grits' patience not to toss the woman over his shoulder and drag her out of the apartment to the safe house. Did she not see what kind of danger she was in? Honestly, he wasn't sure what she was more scared of—the guy with the knife, or maybe it was the thought of being stuck with a stranger for days. Either way, he wasn't paid to wonder why. He was paid to protect.

He moved swiftly to the window, scanning the outside for any sign of threat. Seeing nothing, he turned back just as she handed him his phone, their fingers brushing briefly. "Go pack a bag for a few days." His tone remained gentle but firm, but this dark-haired beauty rankled him by pushing back.

She crossed her arms defiantly. "It's only for a few days."

He nodded, trying to mask his concern. He wanted to be free when his team returned, ready for whatever new mission might arise. Still, he couldn't shake the feeling that she'd cause trouble, especially if that gang member he'd taken down was just the beginning.

As she hurriedly packed her belongings, Grits watched anxiously from the window, catching sight of someone lurking nearby, possibly watching her apartment. But Grits didn't trust coincidences. He knew they were being watched. A chill ran down his spine, leaving him with the uneasy sense that trouble was brewing.

He quickly pulled out his phone and dialed, urgency in his voice. "Jesse, we've got trouble."

"Can you get her out of there?"

Grits scanned the area again, spotting only a solitary man watching from the shadows. "I hope so."

"Emily caught us up on what's happened. If you need help, we can create a barrier to get her out."

Honestly, they should've already been gone, but "Miss Bad Kisser" was taking her sweet time. "We'll be out in a bit, but we might have a tail."

"All right. I'll send Daylan over. He lives nearby and can help."

Grits hesitated. No one trusted Daylan after he ratted out Pup and Elena. Pup and Elena's night together in the hotel was a secret they kept under wraps until Daylan arrived unexpectedly. He walked in to find Pup shirtless and Elena looking disheveled, a scene that spoke volumes. Without hesitation, he reported what he'd seen to Jesse once he returned from his trip.

But right now, he needed someone to block this follower, and the brothers would take too long to arrive.

Determination tightened his jaw. "Okay. Send him here."

Leaving the window, he surveyed the apartment.

She'd transformed part of the spacious living area into a makeshift workspace, complete with a desk, printer, and empty space where a laptop had been. His mind drifted to the thief and the cryptic note. Why did that incident seem to awaken such danger? What was she really involved in? The team hadn't shared everything with him. He shrugged off the questions for now. He'd find out soon enough. But first, they had to move.

"Are you ready? We need to go." Urgency sharpened his tone more than he'd wanted. He knew they'd wait for Daylan, but he needed her to get going faster. She didn't need to pack party dresses—just a few days' worth of clothes and toiletries.

"I'm coming." She rolled a large suitcase from what he guessed was her bedroom. She stopped in front of him, a curious look in her eyes. "Will there be food there, or should we pack some?"

Was she serious? It was as if she were planning a picnic. He knew they kept the safe house in Virginia stocked, but it would take a bit of time for Daylan to arrive. He shrugged with a smile tugging at his lips. "Can't hurt to have a little extra."

"Good, because I have leftovers I was about to freeze." She breezed past him toward the kitchen and looked back over her shoulder. "But with two of us, we can finish them."

He hoped she was a good cook because if he was eating leftovers instead of fresh food from the safe house, it had better be worth it. He checked his watch. "What do you have?"

Moving back to the window, he saw Daylan walking down the street as if he didn't have a care in the world. He looked up at the apartment window, and Grits nodded toward the onlooker between the trees. Daylan slowly changed his direction and circled behind the man, who was intently watching Grits watch him. In an instant, the agent had the man in a chokehold and slowly lowered him to the ground, likely knocking him out.

That was their signal. He swiftly dropped the curtain, eyes fixed. "Forget the food. It's time to move."

She emerged from the kitchen clutching a bowl and looked hesitant. "But—"

He impatiently grabbed her suitcase, wheeling it behind him. "That's enough."

She started to speak again, but he interrupted her.

"We have to go now."

He subtly shepherded her out the door and toward his SUV parked on the street in front of her apartment. He kept a keen watch on Daylan, gauging his every move as he fanned the man, who had "fainted," to distract the curious bystanders. "Thank you, Daylan. I owe you one." A gnawing feeling of unease tightened in his stomach.

As he packed her suitcase in the rear of the vehicle, Ava sank into the passenger seat, her hands already cradling a bowl of food.

He cast a quick glance at the streets, always on alert. That seemed to be their only threat.

He slid into the driver's seat, started the engine, and shifted into Drive. The rumble of the SUV seemed to echo his racing thoughts.

"Homemade vegetable beef soup."

He turned to Ava, confused. "What?"

"In the apartment, you asked what I had. Well, I have homemade vegetable beef soup."

This woman was truly unbelievable. Either she was completely oblivious to the danger she was in, or she was desperately searching for a distraction to keep her mind off it. He secretly hoped it was the latter, so he could play along with her game.

"I love homemade soups."

She nodded. "I make all my soups from scratch." Her pride cut through the thick tension in the SUV like a knife. "So, where are we headed exactly?"

Good. That was a safe topic they could discuss. "We have a house in Virginia that's equipped for keeping people safe."

"Virginia? Why so far? I mean, couldn't we just go to a hotel or something?"

Everyone always asked that. Movies had warped reality. "No. The only way out of a hotel room is through the one door. The only other option is my place, but are you willing to stay there?" The thought just now struck him. His place was secure, but it was in town, too exposed, with too many people around. It wouldn't work.

She hesitated, then shook her head. "No thanks. I'll take Virginia."

Grits nodded slowly. "Smart choice."

A thick silence settled between them, heavy with unspoken thoughts. Normally, he cherished quiet moments, but this tension was gnawing at his gut, unsettling his calm. "What did you do to warrant such attention?"

If she wouldn't tell him, he'd turn to Jesse. When he accepted the assignment, only one thing was clear: she needed to be safe. Jesse had mentioned they didn't have much to go on, so perhaps they were just as in the dark as he was. But he'd said Emily had caught them up on what was happening.

Then, Ava explained her job as a cybersecurity analyst, revealing that she was investigating a recent financial data breach when she discovered an encrypted message hidden in the code. "While I can't say for certain if it's related, it's quite a coincidence."

"Who did you tell about this 'message'?"

She hesitated for a moment before responding, "I called the FTC—Federal Trade Commission—since breaches fall under their jurisdiction. But when they brushed me off, I went straight to the FBI."

"In other words, you didn't keep it a secret."

She turned to him abruptly, her eyes locking onto his with intense focus. "Why would I? It was an anomaly that needed reporting—something that could jeopardize the entire investigation. Remember, I'm here solely for the bank's interests. If I crack the case, I report it to the FTC, and while they might not like everything I say, they accept the data."

Grits snorted, a smirk tugging at his lips. "They probably dislike it. Any luck tracking down where the breach started?"

"Not yet." Then she changed the topic. "By the way, Em mentioned you had a card I could use to buy a new laptop."

He glanced at her, recalling the theft. "Do you really need one?"

She nodded, a quick, decisive movement. "Absolutely. I need to finish my work, and I plan to decrypt that message before long."

Her voice held a fierce determination that set off

warning bells in his mind. Still, he couldn't argue that she had important work that could be done remotely. "Devon will handle the decryption. No need to stress about it." He wondered whether Emily had involved Devon yet, and if not, he was ready to step in.

They continued their journey in silence, and darkness fell. The weight of unasked questions hung in the air. Grits had a dozen of them bubbling up, but he knew to wait until she focused on the data.

Was the trouble about the message she uncovered or the fact that she was investigating the breach itself? And how had anyone known what she was up to? Well, aside from her revealing it to the FTC and FBI, those disclosures alone might be enough to raise red flags. If a rogue element was out there, spilling secrets to the government was the best move to get the word out.

As their vehicle rolled onto the long, winding driveway leading to the Virginia safe house, a chill ran down his spine. Something was off. He could feel it, but couldn't quite put his finger on what. Maybe it was the uncertainty—the not knowing the why—that left his stomach in knots, stirring a restless, uneasy feeling inside.

When a bullet hit the SUV, adrenaline surged through him. "Get down!"

He slammed on the brakes, yanked the vehicle into Reverse, and forced the trembling woman's head lower. The engine roared as he reversed furiously, heart pounding, praying the shooter wouldn't put a bullet through his skull. Silence returned briefly—no more gunfire—but he knew better than to breathe easy.

"What's happening?" Ava's trembling voice pierced the sudden quiet, tugging at his heart.

"Someone's shooting at us." He realized she might not have caught the sharp clang of metal for what it had been, but he definitely had.

Pushing the accelerator harder, he swung onto the deserted highway, headlights cutting through the night. He kept a wary eye on the rearview mirror, tense for any sign of pursuit, but the empty road remained silent.

Once they finally made it to safety, he gently told her she could sit up.

"What happened?"

He couldn't believe she was asking that again. Hadn't she heard him the first time? He glanced at her, noticing her trembling hands clutching the bowl of soup in her lap. His voice softened as he replied, "Someone shot at us."

She shook her head, her brow furrowing. "Maybe it was something else."

His chest clenched at her innocent attempt to dismiss the danger. She didn't deserve the chaos that had been thrown her way.

"No, I'm certain it was a bullet."

She turned toward him, eyes filled with questions. "How did they know we'd be there?"

That question echoed in his mind. How indeed? Someone had shared their destination with the wrong person. Was it deliberate or accidental? Either way, it spelled trouble, and now he had to decide what to do with her, especially since he no longer trusted HIS to keep their location secret.

CHAPTER FIVE

Ava sat in shock, her body frozen in place. All she could do was clutch that damn bowl of soup, her fingertips trembling. Someone had shot at them. Her mind raced. Why were people trying to kill her?

It all pointed back to the secret message she'd uncovered. She'd never had trouble solving a data breach solo before, but now, it was clear that someone desperately didn't want her to decrypt it. With danger closing in, a stranger she didn't know or trust stood guard beside her.

Trust? Ava rarely trusted anyone. If at all. Yet, right now, she had no choice. Grits had saved her twice today. He was serious, focused, and unwavering—a true protector in this chaos that was now her life.

His steely determination shot through her like an arrow, straightening her spine and filling her with resolve. With him standing steadfastly beside her, fear seemed to melt away, replaced by a fierce sense of purpose. Her mind raced as she prepared to decrypt the ominous message, already strategizing about the equipment and software that would be crucial, not just for her role as an analyst, but to unravel the dangerous puzzle threatening her safety.

It was painfully obvious that her adversaries meant business. They were serious about silencing her. Undeterred, she steadied herself for the battle ahead, determined to expose the truth and put an end to their sinister plans once and for all.

Ava turned to Grits, her brow furrowing with curiosity. "Where are we headed now?" She still wasn't ready to go to his place. It felt too…intimate. They needed a safe, neutral place.

Grits flicked her a quick glance. "How are you? Are you okay?"

He kept darting glances between her and the road, making her uneasy.

"I'm fine." Though doubt tugged at her. Was she really? She hadn't been hurt, so that was something.

He nodded. "Uh-huh." As he focused back on the road, the silence grew heavy with unspoken questions. Then he startled her with, "I don't know."

Confused, she stared at him, her brow furrowing. "What?"

"You asked where we're going. I'm not sure yet."

She inhaled sharply. That wasn't good. "Do you think someone at your agency ratted us out?" The words slipped out before she could stop them, and a cold dread crept in. It made sense. If this were a secluded safe house, only HIS knew the destination.

Her mind flickered to Em. Was she safe? Was she okay? Had some madman infiltrated the agency, putting them all in danger?

"Em—" The name escaped before she could rein it in. Her throat tightened, and the question hovered, unspoken but heavy with fear.

He seemed to sense her unspoken question and gently placed a hand on her arm, the contact sending a jolt through her.

"I'm sure she's okay."

His fingers left her arm, leaving her feeling unsure what to think about the contact, then quickly reached for the cell he'd dropped into the console at the start of their journey. With a swift press of his speed dial, he activated Bluetooth, his eyes locking onto hers. She widened her eyes, eager for answers, and he pressed a finger to his lips, silently urging her to stay quiet.

Her heart pounded. She'd stay silent if it meant finding out if Em was safe. The line clicked, and a man's voice answered from the other end.

"Are you at the safe house?"

"About that—"

At Grit's hesitation, the man on the other end nearly shouted, "What?"

"Someone was waiting to ambush us."

Silence for a moment, then "What?"

"Exactly what I said, Jesse. Someone was there. They took a shot at me as soon as I was in range. I spun around and hit the dirt, racing to put some distance between us. I didn't get a clear look."

So, this was the big brother Em had mentioned so often. The reliable protector she trusted. Her heart leapt at Grits calling him.

"Hang on, I'm getting Devon."

"No!" Grits' near shout made her jump. "From now on, this stays between us. You've got a leak."

"That's not how we work. We're a team."

She remained still, but her insides made her want to move around with anxiety. That's when she realized he hadn't denied the leak comment. His silence spoke volumes. The tension thickened, and she knew everything was about to change.

"Well, now that team is just you and me. If you decide to share, I'll go dark."

Ava wasn't sure what exactly that meant, but she felt a flicker of unease. She really hoped Jesse would keep this just between them, because Em was the only other person she truly trusted.

She reached out and placed her hand softly on his arm. When Grits turned to her, she silently mouthed "Emily," giving him silent permission to confide in her friend.

His gaze locked onto her, so intense it seemed to burn right through her. "And Emily," he finally said.

At those words, a surge of relief washed over her. She wanted to shout for joy. Now she knew she had someone in her corner. Someone she could trust to have her back. Not that she was dismissing Grits' abilities, but she needed Em.

Jesse hesitated. "And Devon. There's no way we can do this without him."

Grits paused, obviously weighing the options, before eventually nodding in agreement. "All right, just the three of you. Please apologize to the other brothers for me."

Jesse ignored his statement and stuck to business.

"Where will you be?"

Grits hesitated briefly, then a slight smile touched his lips. "I'm not sure yet. When I figure it out, I'll let you know." With a final nod, he clicked off the call on the radio console, leaving a sense of unresolved tension hanging in the air.

Ava gazed out at the dark road, noticing they had merged onto an interstate heading south. Her curiosity piqued, she opened her mouth to ask again, "Where are we headed?" but hesitated. His brows knit together in a V, deep in thought, giving away nothing.

She wondered silently where their destination might be, clutching her bowl of soup as the cool spring air seeped into the SUV. It was late, yet her mind buzzed with energy—preoccupied with that elusive code she had uncovered and her plan to decrypt it. What would her life look like once she cracked it? Before she could dwell further, Grits broke her train of thought, pulling her back to the present.

"I have a call to make, and I need you to stay silent, no matter what I say."

She nodded, realizing he couldn't see her while he watched the road. "Okay."

"I mean it, Ava. I might say some things that could ruffle your feathers, but you have to remain quiet."

Nerves assailed her at what he could possibly say to ruffle her feathers. "Okay, I'll stay quiet."

He picked up his phone and scrolled through his contacts. Her eyes fixed on the screen to the name "Celeb." She wondered, what's with the quirky names? Did their parents have a sense of humor, or did they not like each other?

He pushed the call button, and the phone rang sharply, breaking the silence in the SUV. When someone finally answered, she sat up straight, bracing herself for what he might say to "ruffle her feathers."

"Grits, my man. How's it hanging?"

Grits cleared his throat, a hint of amusement in his voice. "You're on speakerphone, jackass."

"Well, hell, man. How was I supposed to know that? Who's on the line? Any of the guys? I miss them already."

"Then, you shouldn't have left HIS to chase Hollywood dreams."

Ava's ears twitched at that. Grits knew someone in Hollywood. Her dream has always been to stroll down Hollywood Boulevard, see the Walk of Fame, and soak in all the city has to offer.

"Naw, man. It's my, uh, new woman."

Ava's breath hitched, and for a moment, she nearly blurted out, "That's a lie," but her silence held firm. She'd promised and knew now what feathers he'd ruffle.

"Wow, man. About time you got someone for yourself. So, is she gonna say 'Hi' to your old buddy?"

"Nope." His response was curt, dismissive.

Ava folded her arms, feeling the sting of rudeness. She'd have loved to say "Hi" without any trouble. Instead, she kept her silence, a mix of hurt and frustration simmering inside.

Celeb chuckled. "All right, spill it. What's up? I'm betting this isn't a social call."

Grits cleared his throat. "Do you still have that cabin

out in the woods near DC?"

"Yeah, I'm trying to sell it. Interested?"

"Not quite. I was thinking more along the lines of borrowing it for a while."

Celeb chuckled again. "A little getaway for the lovers, huh? Sure thing."

Grits paused. "But let's keep this between us. No need for anyone else to know."

"No problem, man. Consider it a secret mission."

"Thanks." Grits ended the call with a quick tap on the radio console.

Her nerves eased a bit, knowing Celeb would keep their location under wraps. She shot him a curious look. "Your woman?"

He turned to look at her. "Told you so." A soft chuckle escaped him.

She fidgeted, picking at an imaginary speck of lint on her light sweater. "Feathers, indeed. Why didn't you just tell him the truth? Haven't you worked with him before?"

He remained silent, and that silence irked her. Then he said, "He'd want to help, and he's been out of the game too long."

"What's he doing in Hollywood?"

"He's a stunt double, and he's done some small roles, as far as I know."

Ava fiddled with the bowl, eyes flickering with interest. "You don't keep up with him?"

Grits shook his head, caught briefly in the headlights that approached. "Naw."

She'd make an effort to stay connected with a friend who moved to Hollywood. She'd visit often, too. But men? They were different…more complicated.

"So, where's this cabin? And does it have plumbing?" She shivered at the thought of camping in a primitive shelter, just a roof to keep out the weather and bugs, with no facilities inside.

He laughed, a deep, resonant sound that seemed to reach into her very soul, stirring emotions she thought were long buried—particularly a pain she'd kept locked away since the day she'd been stood up at the altar. Not now. Not in this moment, and not with this man. Lust flickered within her, a dangerous and tempting ember, but acting on it could jeopardize everything.

"Yeah, it's a beautiful three-bedroom cabin right on a tranquil lake." He used his blinker to change lanes before continuing, "Secluded enough that we'll be safe until you decrypt that file."

That reminder hit her sharply. "I need to order some supplies. How do I do that? You made me leave my cell at my apartment, and the laptop I brought is in the back."

He reached into the console and handed her the phone without hesitation. "Here." Then he pulled his wallet out of his back pocket, flipping it open to reveal a credit card labeled Hamilton Investigation and Security. "Use this."

A sudden chill ran down her spine, a creeping suspicion. "Won't they realize we're using it?"

"Yeah, but Devon is on the team and knows we'll be using it. He's the only one monitoring that. Well, and Em, of course, since it's our money." He chuckled, and she missed the humor.

"I'll need the address."

"It's under Celeb's name in my Contacts."

She hesitated. "This is going to be pretty pricey."

He glanced at her, a devilish smile playing on his lips. "Remember, you're paying it back."

She caught his smile and felt a mix of nerves and determination. Then it clicked. She was also covering their service, even though Em had offered it pro bono. That made her his boss. If she didn't like something, she could demand a change. The realization settled over her, relaxing her and fueling her resolve. As she began scoping out the equipment to end this madness, a newfound sense of control washed over her.

CHAPTER SIX

Grits couldn't believe this shit. He meticulously reviewed all the agents present at HIS at that moment, narrowing it down to only one—Daylan. Could the same guy who'd betrayed his teammates to their boss also be leaking intel to some secret organization hell-bent on ending Ava? The thought ignited a fiery rage in him, making him want to punch the hell out of the gym's punching bag.

It all made sense now. Alpha and Bravo teams were out of the picture. That's how he landed the babysitting gig. Charlie team, as Daylan had claimed, had already dispersed. Which left only one agent: Daylan. Son of a bitch!

Grits' mind raced. He bet they had been headed straight to the safe house after leaving her apartment. No one had to tell him that. It was SOP—standard operating procedure. That confirmed it. He wasn't on HIS side in this fight. And it's never a good sign when someone's put a hole in your prized SUV. That only fanned his fury, stoking his desire for vengeance.

Ava scrolled hurriedly through his phone, her eyes darting for the equipment she needed to decrypt the mysterious message pulsating at the heart of it all. Could she crack it? Or would Devon beat her to it? Either way, with both of them racing against time, they'd be out of this madness before it consumed them.

Once her fear of the shooting had subsided, she had transformed into a true trooper, determined to do whatever it took to solve the puzzle. And damn, she looked good doing it. That made him wonder—was she still a bad kisser? The thought snapped him back to reality. What the hell was he thinking?

She gently set the phone down on the console. "I think I've got everything, but I really hope this place has WI-FI. I need to download a ton of software once I get the equipment set up."

He glanced at her. "When do you think that'll be?" He wasn't always the most patient, especially not when waiting for days to pass.

"Not tomorrow, obviously, since it's nearly midnight. But the day after that, I should be good since I had it all sent next day."

He nodded, relief washing over him. They could manage one day without her working. Additionally, it gave him a bit of time to ensure the area was secure and free of surprises.

She stretched lazily, letting out a slow yawn as her chest pushed subtly against his peripheral vision. He gulped, feeling the tension rise. One day with nothing to do might seem easy, but today it was anything but.

"Why don't you get some rest? I'll wake you when we

reach our destination."

She set the bowl of soup down on the floorboard, clasped her hands in her lap, and twirled her thumbs. "I don't think I can sleep. I keep expecting someone to jump out at us."

His heart ached for her, for her evident fear. After two brutal attempts on her life today, she was holding herself together remarkably well. Yet, he suspected the full weight of it hadn't truly hit her yet.

He reached out, gently stilling her restless thumbs, instantly regretting the warm contact. He quickly withdrew his hand, trying to soothe her with his voice. "It's okay. We're safe now. And it'll be a couple of hours before we get there. Close your eyes, rest for a bit."

She yawned again, eyes half-lidded. "I...I just can't."

A heavy silence filled the cabin. When they finally pulled into a gas station to refuel, Grits smiled. She was already lost in sleep.

He paid at the pump and refueled the SUV, feeling the anticipation build. He wanted to grab snacks for the road, but hesitated. She shouldn't wake up alone in a strange place. Gently, he reached over and woke her. "Ava, time to wake up."

Her eyelids fluttered open, and confusion clouded her chestnut eyes. Suddenly, she jumped, cheeks flushing with embarrassment. "Oh, I fell asleep."

He couldn't help but smile at her bashful reaction. "It's okay. We're almost there. I wanted to get some food, and I didn't want you to wake up alone out here."

She unbuckled her seatbelt and nodded. "Good plan."

Though he didn't need her approval, he appreciated

her confidence. If hearing he's doing well helped her feel better, he'd let her believe it.

After snagging the best snacks and essentials from the little convenience store, they packed up the SUV and hit the road again.

She opened her mouth to ask a question, but he cut her off with a quick, "We're almost there."

She nodded and stole a glance at him. "Good."

He couldn't help but want to chuckle at how business-like she was now—so professional, yet still undeniably adorable.

"Tell me more about your work as an analyst and who you work for?" He kept his eyes fixed on the road and in the rear-view mirror, wary of any surprises this time. He hadn't heard of an employer, and that made him wonder if they had a player out there he didn't know about.

She turned to him. "I work for myself now. I used to be with the government, but the bureaucracy...." He caught her hand's subtle movement, but still refused to look directly at her, partly because she looked breathtaking, especially as she stretched languidly from her nap. Something about her made his thoughts wander dangerously close to a line he didn't want to cross.

"Anyway, I'm hired by companies to do a variety of tasks. One might need me to ensure their encryption can withstand a cyberattack, while another might want me to investigate a breach to understand how their defenses failed. It varies, but essentially, I analyze their networks, software, and systems to find vulnerabilities and keep their data and infrastructure safe."

"Can't these businesses just hire their own analysts?"

She nodded. "They could. Some do. I just supplement what they have on staff. That is, if they can afford it. We're not exactly cheap."

He was impressed by what she could do. He knew Stone was studying to become a cybersecurity analyst to boost his skills at HIS, but he'd never really asked what that role entailed. All he knew was that Stone worked with Devon whenever extra help was needed. He missed having Stone in the field. The man had been rock-solid.

Then a thought suddenly hit him like a bolt of lightning. Could Stone truly be the breach? He wanted to dismiss the idea immediately, but he knew better than to block out any possibilities, especially since they had only let in three trusted individuals. Sure, he trusted the brothers implicitly, but there was always that nagging suspicion that someone might have talked, or maybe they anticipated their next move.

He decided Jesse should look into both men, if he wasn't already. Something told him Jesse wouldn't sit idly by if this leak persisted. The integrity of HIS reputation meant everything to the family. No one was going to tarnish that, nor harm a client.

"So, how much are you going for?" he asked, almost without thinking. Then he caught himself and quickly clarified, "I mean, how much do you charge?"

She waved her hand dismissively. "I know what you meant. It's a steep bill when I do something, but it's worth it."

"Yet, Em says you work nonstop. What are you saving for?"

When she fidgeted and brought her thumb to her

mouth, he realized he'd touched a nerve.

"Never mind. We're here."

He steered onto a dirt road, crunching beneath tires as the landscape shifted from woods to an open clearing, revealing a large log cabin. The few men from Bravo team, who'd been here before, spoke of good times and camaraderie that were now just memories. Luckily, Stone had been on Alpha team, and Daylan was on Charlie team, so neither of them knew about this hidden gem.

Could there be someone secretly feeding false information to the wrong person? Had Charlie's entire team truly left, as he'd heard? He decided to have Jesse verify that. An unknown player might be lurking in the shadows.

"Wow. This is breathtaking." Awe lingered in her voice.

The moonlight shimmered over the water, casting a gentle glow on the cabin and creating a breathtaking scene. "It is."

He shifted the vehicle into Park and turned toward her, his eyes steady. "Now, you stay right here while I go check things out."

She stiffened, her jaw clenched. He could see the fight brewing in her eyes. "You're not leaving me here. I demand you take me with you."

Demand? What kind of craziness was this? His voice was firm but with an edge of surprise. "No. You'll stay right here like a good girl and let me make sure it's safe."

But almost immediately, he realized he'd spoken the wrong words, regret flashing through him as the tension thickened.

"Good girl?" Her voice jumped an octave as she repeated the words he desperately wished he'd never spoken. "Good girl? Listen here, mister. I am your boss on this little…adventure, and I expect you to keep me with you, not leave me for some stranger to snatch."

What the actual fuck was she spouting? "First, you're not my boss on this adventure, and second, no one's going to snatch you." But then he hesitated, reconsidering. Maybe someone was lurking. Maybe Celeb had told someone, but who? He hadn't been close to Stone or known Daylan.

He changed his mind. It was safer to keep her close. "Okay, but you stay behind me and do exactly as I say. If I say run, you run until you drop. Do you understand?"

She gave him a playful mock salute. "Yes, sir, drill sergeant, sir."

He shook his head, chuckling at her quick wit. This was shaping up to be one interesting assignment.

He checked his Glock one last time, then slid it back into its holster with a sense of readiness. Although he was prepared, there was still gear in the back that had to wait. Clearing the area was the top priority.

Knowing exactly where Celeb kept the spare key, Grits headed toward the rock pile behind the cabin. Darkness cloaked the surroundings, making it hard to see what he needed. Reluctantly, he pulled out his phone's flashlight, praying it wouldn't reveal their position to any lurking, prying eyes.

He located the fake rock, retrieved the key, and switched off his phone's light. Tucking the device into his pocket, he took Ava's hand gently and tugged. "Come on."

To his surprise, she followed without resistance, her grip on his hand firm. Prepared to drop the key at a moment's notice if he needed to draw his weapon, Grits inched up the stairs toward the cabin, every sense on high alert.

He leaned close to her, voice just above a whisper. "Stay here and let me check it out."

She stiffened instantly, and he almost expected her to resist. Instead, she hesitated, then dropped his hand and nodded, melting into the shadows of the front porch's corner, eyes fixed on the darkness.

Good girl. This time, he was relieved he hadn't voiced those words aloud.

He peered through the open windows, annoyance flickering at the lack of curtains or blinds. Celeb had ensured the lake view remained unobstructed. They'd have to make do.

Seeing nothing move, he slowly unlocked the door. One last glance at where Ava was hidden, and he slipped inside. The cabin was dim, but he gradually navigated the familiar layout, accidentally bumping into the kitchen island.

Feeling certain the cabin was empty, he headed back to the front to find Ava—only she was gone.

CHAPTER SEVEN

Ava's eyes locked onto the terror etched across Grits' face. Without hesitation, she stepped boldly from the shadows, voice trembling, and she pointed. "There—" she began, but the words caught in her throat, shaken to her core.

Grits looked up, relief flooding his rugged features. "Thank God." But his expression hardened as he turned sharply. "Why the hell did you move?"

Ava pointed across the porch. "Spi—Spider." The word finally escaped her lips, a victory in her struggle.

Grits' jaw clenched. "Woman, I told you to stay put. There are people out there aiming to kill you. If you have to handle a simple spider—" he paused, eyes narrowing. "—then so be it."

Ava shook her head fiercely, voice edged with desperation. "Arachnophobia." Her voice was barely above a whisper, but the tension lingered, thick and unrelenting.

He heaved a heavy sigh, pinching the bridge of his nose as if trying to stave off the madness. "What have I gotten myself into?" His words were tinged with a mix of frustration and curiosity.

Grits' low, grating voice cut through the moment, stirring irritation in her.

She planted her hands firmly on her hips. "It's a real thing." Her eyes blazed with conviction.

He looked at her, lips thinning into a narrow line.

She rushed to explain. "I was bitten once when I was ten and got really sick and almost died."

"Brown recluse? Black widow?"

She nodded. "They think so. I was bitten while I slept. So, that's why—"

He shook his head. "Don't worry about it. I understand. My sister has it. She got it from that damn movie."

Her breath hitched, deflating the tension. "Oh." She paused, realizing their whispers echoed through the quiet cabin. "Is it safe?"

He studied her face for a beat, then nodded slowly. "Yeah. Let's get you inside." Without waiting, he gently guided her into the cabin and flicked on the lights.

She scoffed quietly. If he'd just turned on the porch light, he'd have seen her standing there. Her annoyance bubbled beneath the surface. She'd gotten a lecture from her own employee, and that rankled more than she cared to admit.

It wasn't just that he was an employee. Somehow, she was starting to trust him—a little. Today, he had gone above and beyond to keep her safe, risking his own life each time he stepped between her and danger. Yet, her stubbornness held firm. She valued her independence too much to let vulnerability creep in, especially not from a blond, handsome stranger who swore he would protect her with his life.

"What's going on in that head of yours?"

She jumped, caught off guard. "Oh." She waved her hand dismissively. "Nothing."

"Uh-huh." He guided her through the cozy cabin with gentle confidence. He pointed out each feature, stopping briefly to designate which bedroom would be hers. Before letting her settle in, he meticulously checked the window locks and closed the blinds, ensuring everything was secure. At least the bedrooms had blinds, she thought, remembering the vast, unshielded picture window at the front of the cabin—huge enough to frame a stunning landscape or an unwelcome stranger.

It had been a long, exhausting day.

He glanced at her with genuine concern. "Are you hungry? Want to grab a bite before you rest?"

Her stomach rumbled at the mention of food, momentarily distracting her from her fatigue. "Oh, the soup." She remembered the leftovers she'd left in the SUV.

He stopped her gently, a reassuring smile on his face. "I'll get it all."

She hesitated. "But I can help—"

He shook his head, voice firm but kind. "No, thank you. I've got it. Someone might put you in their crosshairs, and I've risked enough lives today. Besides, you need to rest."

There it was again—that commanding voice asserting he believed he was in control. But today, she was too exhausted to argue. Let him wheel the luggage and unpack the leftovers from the SUV. She just wanted to lie down and take a breath.

"How dusty do you think this place is?" She hadn't noticed any dust, but she'd only taken a quick look. Dust usually meant spiders. "I really don't want to sleep in a dust cloud."

He chuckled, a warm sound that seemed to soothe her weary soul. "He keeps this place cleaned weekly, just in case he wants to invite his Hollywood friends for a quick getaway." Then he looked pointedly at her. "He also has it sprayed regularly for critters."

"Oh," was all she could manage about the thoughtful spraying. She was still awestruck that he knew someone who'd acted in Hollywood. She couldn't wait to meet Celeb.

Then she wondered, when would she actually meet him? It wasn't like she and Grits would become BFFs after this, nor did she expect him to invite her when Celeb was in town. The anticipation buzzed in her mind.

"I'll be right back." He turned to leave her in the bedroom she'd call home for the next couple of days until she finally decrypted that damn message.

As her thoughts drifted back to the message and the new equipment she had eagerly ordered, she lounged comfortably on her bed, clad in her jeans and light sweater. Just as her eyelids began to flutter shut, she suddenly sat up with a start, pacing the room anxiously until Grits appeared at the doorframe, suitcase in hand.

Eager to change and catch some rest, she politely declined dinner when he offered. "No, but you enjoy the soup."

"Are you sure?"

She sensed the worry in his voice, and it touched her heart.

She nodded, a tentative smile flickering across her face. "I'm sure. I think I'll call it a night." Relieved, she made her way to her suitcase, eager to escape the tension that hung between them. He loomed there, filling the doorway with an imposing presence. Though he was taller by about six or seven inches, it was as if a giant had taken form in the light spilling around him.

"That sounds like a wise idea." He turned and left her standing there, her mind racing with unspoken thoughts. Then it hit her—she was genuinely attracted to him. A sharp groan escaped her as she closed the door behind him with a soft click, her mind a whirlwind of confusion. This was complicated, and she wasn't sure she was ready for where her feelings might lead.

Rummaging through her suitcase—she'd unpack tomorrow—she slipped into a pair of shorts and a T-shirt, leaving her bra on. She wasn't about to parade around him braless, especially not with the chill still lingering in the March air, making her acutely aware of her not-so-endowed figure. She hated walking around showing her headlights on a cool day.

Climbing into the cozy queen-sized bed, she immediately pulled the covers back, checking for spiders with a quick glance—finding none, she sank into the softness. A silent prayer of gratitude escaped her lips for surviving that day, and she drifted into a light sleep.

The gentle morning light seeped through the edges of

the blinds, gradually waking her.

It took her a moment to realize where she was and why. She jolted up, her gaze rapidly scanning the room as though an assassin might be hiding in the shadows.

"Grits." The name slipped from her lips in a soft, almost wistful sigh. She wondered if he'd slept as peacefully as she had, the kind of sleep that leaves you floating in a calm haze. Rising from bed, she approached the window, opening the blinds to reveal that the morning had already unfurled into a bright, bustling day. A ripple of worry clenched her stomach that she'd overslept. Yet, then she remembered that she had no pressing plans for the day. The equipment delivery wasn't until tomorrow, leaving her free to relax—if only her assailant would grant her that luxury.

Her mind spiraled into a whirlwind of scenarios, each more perilous than the last, where Grits appeared like a guardian angel, rescuing her just in the nick of time, and giving her that familiar stern lecture about staying put or following his orders. Bossy much? She rolled her eyes at her own thoughts, a flicker of amusement breaking through her anxiety.

Opening her suitcase, she took a moment to hang her clothing in the small closet and carefully place her underthings in the dresser. The cozy room exuded a quiet charm that made her feel at ease. She could see why Celeb loved the place.

Her thoughts were interrupted by a sudden knock on her door. She hesitated, nearly asking, "Who is it?" but then remembered who it was. Or was it? An assassin knocking? The idea sent a shiver down her spine. Could he have overpowered Grits? Her heart pounded at the thought of being alone with someone potentially dangerous on her tail.

"Grits?" Her voice wavered, trembling with uncertainty, wishing whoever was on the other side hadn't heard her hesitation.

"Yeah. I've got breakfast if you're hungry."

She relaxed at Grits' commanding voice. How long had she slept? She glanced at her smartwatch, now dead, a sinking feeling in her chest. She'd obviously slept longer than he had. Or…had he even slept at all? Who was watching them while he was asleep? That question made her heart race faster. Would she ever truly sleep again, or was she trapped in a nightmare she couldn't wake from?

"Let me get dressed, then I'll be there." Her voice remained steady despite the flutter in her chest. There was a brief silence before she heard his retreating footsteps. How come she hadn't heard him approaching? Was he that stealthy, or had he simply let her hear him leave her alone? She couldn't decide.

She hurried into the en-suite bathroom, then quickly pulled on a long-sleeved T-shirt—perfect for the cool morning. She knew she could always roll up the sleeves when the afternoon heat kicked in. After slipping into her jeans, she sank into a lonely armchair to put on her tennis shoes, determined not to run barefoot if they had to leave in a hurry.

Back in the bathroom, she ran her fingers through her shoulder-length hair, battling the humidity that had turned her natural wave into frizz. With a sigh, she pulled it back into a neat ponytail, then scrubbed her face and applied moisturizer. The morning ritual calmed her.

She was grateful that he'd given her enough time to pack her essentials. She couldn't imagine facing this journey without her toothbrush and toothpaste. After one last look, she headed toward the bedroom door, ready to face whatever lay ahead.

The spacious open cabin, with its soaring high ceilings and expansive layout, was a masterpiece of architecture that left Ava breathless. Intricate beams crisscrossed overhead, adding a majestic touch that heightened the room's grandeur and charm. Every detail, from the craftsmanship of the beams to the flood of natural light streaming in, created an atmosphere of awe and wonder.

She made her way to the open kitchen, where Grits greeted her with a warm smile and offered her an omelet and toast.

He shrugged. "I wasn't sure what you liked, but most everyone loves cheese omelets."

She loved omelets of any kind. "Thank you." She picked up the fork beside her plate and took a bite. It was delicious. Something extra had been added to keep it from being bland.

She moaned. "What did you—"

Grits shook his head with a mischievous grin. "It's a family secret."

Well, it was a family secret she'd had to pry out of him at some point. After finishing her breakfast, she took a slow sip of her coffee. She was thankful she drank it black because he hadn't offered cream or sugar. Though she secretly craved vanilla creamer, she indulged only once a week. Her sweet tooth was too strong to justify daily indulgence. Not precisely a health fanatic, she still aimed to eat right, saving herself from the grueling two-hour workout some former colleagues swore by. Better to spend that time reading or working.

She set her coffee cup on the counter where they'd eaten. "What's next?"

Grits grimaced. "We wait for your equipment, and pray Devon's faster than you."

She bristled at the remark but let it slide. "Do you really think he can help?" While her gut told her she should find the breach herself and decipher that encrypted message, having Devon's help could be a lifesaver—in more ways than one.

CHAPTER EIGHT

Grits couldn't believe it. He had an entire day with nothing but time to spend with Ava.

How was he supposed to manage keeping her safe all alone? His sleep had been restless the night before, haunted by the fear that someone might be lurking in the shadows. Trust was already fraying. He couldn't rely on the agents right now. Someone had leaked the location of the safe house, whether by mistake or betrayal. It had happened, and he couldn't accept it. Someone's days were numbered at HIS. Secretly, he hoped it was Daylan, but he wasn't sure why. They just didn't get along. Daylan rubbed most of the agents the wrong way, and their fragile trust was hanging by a thread.

Recalling that she had asked a question, he nodded confidently. "Devon is the best there is." He caught the flicker of bristling on her face, but he dismissed it. Devon truly was exceptional. But had she ever shown her own skills? Was she an elite hacker like Devon? There was too much Devon learned lurking in the shadows of the digital world for him not to have hacked into someone's system now and then.

She nodded, a small smile curling on her lips. "Good." Without a word, she rose and stretched, causing her chest to catch his eye—an unintentional yet irresistible invitation. He knew it wasn't meant to tease, but there they were, asking for his touch.

"Since you cooked, I'll clean." She grabbed both of their plates and headed toward the sink. He could help, of course, but there were things he needed to check on, and one of which definitely wasn't her enticing, fine ass.

This was shaping up to be one of the trickiest assignments he'd ever undertaken. The fragile balance he'd hoped to establish through this forced proximity was already falling apart—at least on his side. He had no clue how she truly felt about him, and that uncertainty was what made the whole thing even more complicated.

Then he wanted to slap himself mentally. What the hell was he thinking? Just because he desired her didn't mean he had to act on it—especially now, on assignment. She was their client, after all. Yet, he couldn't help but notice that many other agents had ended up marrying their clients, turning fleeting encounters into forever connections.

That thought slammed into him like a bucket of cold water, sobering his lustful thoughts. Marriage? Not in his plans. He couldn't promise forever, not with the scars he carried inside. Those wounds were too deep to risk opening up to anyone.

He cleared his throat, then slowly turned away from her, standing upright. "I'll check the perimeter." A long walk along the property would serve two purposes. It would reacquaint him with the terrain and ensure it was as secure as possible.

He needed help, but who could he trust? Celeb was out of the question. This was too dangerous. And waiting for her to get her equipment? That thought made his skin crawl. Every second wasted was more time for the bad guys to find them.

Once he stepped into the brisk morning air, he took a deep breath, savoring the crisp, clean scent—something he truly missed growing up on the beach. He also missed the ocean's endless horizon, but now a vast lake filled its place. With a sense of routine, he reached for his phone, pulling it from his pocket as he stepped off the porch of the cabin.

"Grits, how are you?"

Jesse was always straight to the point with him, and he appreciated that no-nonsense approach. He wasn't one for chit-chat, and he had a feeling Ava would be the talkative type today, which wouldn't work for him.

"We're safe. Listen, I need help. Can one of the brothers give me relief at night?"

"Where are you?" Jesse's clipped voice sent shivers down many a man's spine, but Grits let it roll off him.

He hesitated, searching for the right words, knowing he couldn't give away their exact location. "Let's just say I'm off the grid."

The line fell silent for a moment before Jesse spoke again. "Everyone's tied up. The only one I can spare is Daylan."

Grits rubbed the back of his neck nervously, weighing his options. He was desperate for help, but trusting

Daylan felt like a gamble. "Are you sure there isn't anyone else?" He scanned the area for possible threats.

"What's the problem with Daylan? He even comes with a K9."

Grits knew the handler was capable, yet a gnawing suspicion lingered—did he expose their location? "I don't trust him." There, he'd admitted it, his voice thick with tension.

A heavy silence settled between them, unnerving in its silent intensity, until Jesse's steady voice broke it. "I trust him. That should be enough."

Grits hesitates, the doubt still clawing at him. "But what if he's the one who leaked our location? If that's the case, sharing where we are now would be reckless."

"I know Daylan's had his fair share of struggles trying to fit in, but he's someone we trust. I don't believe he's the one who shared your location."

"Then who?"

Jesse hesitated, his silence hanging in the air, and Grits felt the weight of unspoken truths pressing down on him. "I'll let you know when I'm sure. From now on, only share your info with me, and only on this line."

He knew he could do that, but a part of him hesitated —giving out the address felt risky. Daylan and Jesse needed it, though. Well, Jesse might not need it, but someone had to know where they were in case he missed checking in and their bodies needed to be found.

"Grits—"

"Yeah, Old Man?" he responded, slipping back into their tactical callsigns for Jesse as the big boss.

Jesse chuckled softly. "Trust me."

A wave of relief mixed with anxiety washed over him. He understood what that meant—help from Daylan was his only shot.

"Okay." He gave Jesse the address.

Before he disconnected, a sudden thought struck him like lightning. "How's Devon faring with that message?"

The silence that followed was heavy, each second pounding in Grits' chest, making his heart race. Then came the devastating news—

"Devon's in the hospital. He'll be there for a couple of days." Jesse hesitated, his voice tinged with worry. "Without his laptop."

Shit. Shit. Shit. Grits clenched his fists, knowing Devon was their best shot at cracking that code. If he succeeded, Grits would be free from this deadly assignment. And more importantly, Ava's safety depended on it.

But a nagging question prickled at him. Why was her safety the most important thing right now? But he couldn't dwell on it now.

"What's wrong with him?"

"He had a mild heart attack."

"No shit?" Grits couldn't believe it. The Hamiltons were fitness nuts, especially Rylee, Devon's husband. They worked out. They did everything right. "How is he?" Obviously not good if he was still in the hospital.

"He'll be fine. They just want to run more tests, run up the bill, you know how they get."

"No laptop?"

"Rylee's orders, although the doctor agreed. He said Devon had too much stress."

He probably did with all the teams he had to keep track of, but that's why Stone had started helping so long ago. Back after Boss and Sugar had been captured. Damn. That seemed ages ago. Yet, Devon had always kept the lead, only allowing Stone to take it whenever he couldn't be available for some reason—which was almost never.

Jesse's voice cut through his thoughts. "I've got Stone working on it. He might surprise you."

Grits knew Stone had mad computing skills. But was he up to the task? With time running out, he had no choice but to find out.

"Thank you." Grits ended the call quietly. Concern for Devon washed over him, hoping he would heal soon. But would things change now? Would Stone take on a greater role? He'd have to because Grits couldn't see Rylee allowing Devon to work as much as he had before.

Having precisely walked the perimeter, he paused on the porch, captivated by the breathtaking landscape unfolding before him. The lake stretched out endlessly, its surface mirror-like and shimmering in a vivid shade of blue.

He heard the door creak open behind him, and instantly he knew it was Ava. The subtle scent of her perfume wafted through the air—a surprising choice for someone on the run, yet he understood she had time to pack. Or maybe she simply didn't know what to expect.

"It's beautiful, isn't it?"

He nodded, a slow, knowing smile curving his lips. "It is. That's exactly why Celeb won't sell it. He jokingly talks about putting it on the market, but deep down, he'll keep this treasure forever. It's his sanctuary."

She moved gracefully toward the porch swing, and his pulse quickened. What was she doing out in the open like this? Then it hit him—he'd secured the area. Still, part of him wondered if he'd missed something.

Moving to sit in a chair nearby, he settled himself with a quiet resolve. "We have someone coming to help." His tone carried a weight that made her question him.

"What aren't you telling me?"

How could she read him so quickly? They'd only just met, yet he felt exposed like an open book she was eager to read. Most of his adult life, he'd been told he was hard to crack. Now, faced with her piercing gaze, it was clear he'd have to be honest. "I don't trust him." The words hung heavy in the air. He also didn't trust Daylan around Ava, but he kept that part to himself, guarded and silent.

She stiffened slightly, and he could tell he wasn't winning any points by making her uncomfortable. "Why is he even coming if you don't trust him? It's my life, and I'd feel better knowing I can trust him to vanquish the bad guys."

He chuckled softly at her phrase, "vanquish the bad guys," before his expression deepened with seriousness. "Because Jesse trusts him."

She nodded thoughtfully. "Ah, Jesse. The alpha of the family."

It was clear Emily had described her family perfectly. He nodded in agreement. "Yes, he is."

She hesitated. "When will he get here? The help, I mean?"

He knew precisely who she was referring to but chose not to comment. He checked his watch, which needed charging. "About five hours." It was nearly a four-and-a-half-hour drive to their destination, and he expected Daylan to leave immediately.

She looked down at her empty wrist, prompting him to wonder if she had a charger for her watch.

He'd noticed her watch the first time he saw her when he'd catalogued her for his memory. Now he remembered that first sight of her with her dark, raven hair framing her face…her mesmerizing chestnut eyes… and her brilliant smile that seemed to light up a room.

"What are we going to do until then?"

Grits had an idea, but quickly dismissed it. Sex wasn't an option—too risky, too complicated. "There are books inside." He forced a smile. "Didn't you bring an old laptop?" He hesitated to admit that Devon wasn't working on the code. His primary concern was keeping her spirits high as long as possible.

She nodded in agreement, and her excitement bled out. "I did."

Just as she was about to stand, Grits caught himself, surprising both of them by asking a question instead of letting her walk away. "Are you from Baltimore?" He was cautious not to make assumptions, given that they had many transplants.

She nodded again, a faint smile on her face. "All my life, except for college and work."

"Where did you go to college?" Grits pressed, the words tumbling out before he could stop them. It was strange—these questions felt almost instinctual. Perhaps it was because he didn't have a detailed client profile to work from, unlike his experience with general operations. But he knew it was more than that.

"MIT."

He whistled softly, genuinely impressed. "Damn, MIT. That's impressive. What about work? You mentioned before you worked for the government or something before going solo." Or was that Emily who told him? He needed to straighten out his facts.

Their conversation hung in the air, lively and full of unspoken curiosity. They had a small, unexpected spark of connection in an uncertain moment.

He had to cut it, so he stood. "I'll check the pantry for lunch and dinner options. Sorry, we don't have anything fresh. I'll send Daylan to the store as soon as he arrives." He considered ordering delivery but quickly dismissed the idea. Most likely, no one would deliver this far out, and he didn't want anyone else to know someone was here.

"Let's go inside." He didn't want to leave her outside unprotected, but he couldn't stay in that intimate moment.

She hesitated, then said, "Okay. I'll see what I can do on my old laptop. I don't think it'll be much, but I can try."

Before she could walk past him, he halted her where they were nearly touching. The faint scent of her perfume wafted to him. He wanted to lean down and kiss her, take her, make her his, and that scared the hell out of him. He had to maintain focus.

So, he did the only thing he could think of. He leaned in to kiss her.

CHAPTER NINE

Ava's heart pounded as she watched Grits inch closer, his intentions clear in his slow, deliberate movements. She hesitated, longing for the moment to last forever, but just when she thought he might actually kiss her, he paused, standing tall and leaving her aching for what might have been.

She stood there, her pulse racing, unsure if it was disappointment or relief flowing through her.

Grits turned abruptly, walking away toward the lake, leaving her on the porch.

She paused, about to call after him. Maybe it was just a moment—a reckless, fleeting spark—and nothing more.

It was frustrating to be attracted to a man and feel powerless to act on it. She'd been drawn to men before, but circumstances never allowed her to do anything about it, at least, not in a cozy setting like this. Her mind lingered on that thought, and suddenly, something sparked. Were killers really trying to find them? Her heartbeat quickened. She had to crack the code.

Driven by full-fledged adrenaline, she darted into her

bedroom, snatching her old, clunky laptop and a notepad and pen. The old laptop didn't have all the latest bells and whistles, but maybe—just maybe—it was enough. Who knew? Perhaps she'd get lucky.

She carried her laptop and charger to the kitchen bar, eagerly searching for the plug. When she finally found it and powered up her old baby, her heart skipped a beat at the sight of active Wi-Fi in the house—until she discovered it was password-protected. Disappointment hit, but she turned her attention to the front of the cabin, gazing toward the lake where Grits stood peacefully. She knew she'd have to wait since she wasn't about to chase after him or shout for some villain to find her. Yet, patience was definitely not her strong suit.

Instead, she started jotting down everything she knew about the breach and the code. The bank had called her just two days before her life spiraled out of control, but she hadn't had a chance to process it. Suddenly, the front door swung open and shut. She stiffened, eyes clenched shut. Please let it be Grits.

He cleared his throat. "Don't worry. It's just me."

She spun around on her barstool just as he strode directly toward her. An electric charge seemed to ripple through the air—something unspoken, yet fiercely palpable.

Without a word, he grasped her hand, lifting her from her seat with a gentle yet commanding force. A low groan escaped him as he pulled her close, one hand softly threading into her hair, the other gripping her waist as if he'd been dreaming of this moment forever.

Their lips met in a passionate meld that was slow and

intense—a fiery promise sealed in heat. He kissed her like he couldn't bear to stop, as if the world behind them was ablaze, and in that instant, she was the only thing that mattered.

His tongue delicately and cautiously dared to explore the soft contours of her lips, seeking entry with gentle insistence. Ava's breath hitched, and she responded with a welcoming warmth, parting her lips slightly to invite him further into her embrace, eager and open to his tender advance.

When they finally pulled apart, breathless, foreheads pressed together, he whispered, "You really should be sitting on this side of the bar so you can see the door."

"Oh" was all she managed.

Then he lifted her and deposited her in a chair he deemed safer. She was eager not to get caught off guard, so she let it slide. Yet, she knew that once she focused on her computer, everything else would fade away, leaving her vulnerable in the most unpredictable moments.

He moved her equipment in front of her, then stepped to the front of the kitchen bar. His gaze swept over the entire room as he rested his forearms on the counter like nothing had just happened between them. "Now, tell me everything about this code."

Ava clasped her hands together, readying herself to tell the story. "It all began with a breach at First Regions Bank of Maryland. They brought me in to investigate, and I uncovered the leak of personal and financial data."

He nodded, as if coaxing her to continue.

She cleared her throat, the retelling bringing her current, dangerous situation to life. "But that was just the beginning. As I pored over the tangled code, I stumbled upon an anomaly. It shouldn't have been there and wasn't the cause of the breach."

She looked at him with satisfaction, telling the story as succinctly as she could.

"That's it?"

She nodded. "That's it."

He stood tall, rubbing his chin thoughtfully. "How can you be sure that's really a secure message, leading to something sinister?"

She hesitated, surprised by his question. Hadn't she just explained everything clearly? "Because cryptology was my minor at MIT and because someone is trying to kill me."

Finally saying those last words out loud sent a shiver of fear slicing through her. Her heart pounded as the reality sank in. She'd never been in anyone's crosshairs before. Who really had? But still, the fear terrified her. All her bravado evaporated in an instant.

He seemed to read her thoughts, as if seeing inside her soul, and attempted to soothe her with a calm voice. "It's okay. I'm here, and soon someone else will be, too. You've got HIS working on the code with you."

That caught her attention. "That reminds me. I need to speak with Devon about what I've found and what he's discovered so far."

Grits looked uncomfortable, and the controlled agent shifted slightly—just for a second. But it was enough to give her a clue that something wasn't right.

She didn't wait for him to respond, her voice slicing through the tension. "What is it? What aren't you telling me?" Her words were sharp, urgent.

Then, the words hit her like a punch to the stomach. "There's no easy way to say this, but Devon's in the hospital."

Her heart skipped a beat, and worries about Devon and her safety flooded her mind. "Is he okay?" She knew deep down that it was a stupid question. If he were in the hospital, he wasn't okay.

Grits nodded decisively. "He will be. But right now, Joe Stone is on it."

Thinking back to Emily's description of the men, she nodded again, a spark of recognition in her eyes. "I remember Em telling me about him. He used to be an agent in the field, wasn't he?"

"Yeah." Grits stepped back to the wall, leaning against it.

"What made him change course?"

"Family matters" was all he said, then quickly shifted the subject. "He'll help. But right now, can you do anything with that laptop?"

She shook her head, frustration swirling. "Not much. I can work on the breach a bit, but I need more—Oh, I need the WI-FI password."

Grits stepped forward, his movements purposeful as he rummaged through a drawer beneath the kitchen cabinet. His hand emerged with a small, crumpled piece of paper, which he carefully handed to her, his smile knowing. "Here you go."

She hesitated for a moment, her eyes widening as she instinctively clasped it to her chest, a treasure more valuable than gold. With bated breath, she looked at the paper, glimpsed its contents, and then eagerly entered the information into her computer, anticipation tingling in the air.

"Bingo!" she exclaimed as her laptop connected to the internet. "Wait, if I log into my cloud, won't someone catch it?" She hesitated, unaware of who their enemies might be.

Grits shrugged casually. "Let's get Stone on the line." He pulled out his phone and hit a speed dial with practiced ease.

As he waited for the connection, his eyes briefly studied her, not in a flirtatious way, but with sharp calculation, taking in her attire and appearance. Was he evaluating her in case he needed to give the police her description if she went missing? A cold shiver ran down her spine.

"Hey, Stone. We've got a question for you."

Hearing only one side of the conversation, she silently huffed, slightly annoyed. He had said "we," implying others were involved.

"Yeah. She's here. Where the hell else would she be?" He shot her a quick glance.

Then, a pause. "Oh."

He put the call on speaker. "He wants to talk to you."

The tension in the air was thick as the situation rapidly unfolded, unpredictable and charged with urgency. Her shoulders snapped straight, and a spark lit in her eyes. She was eager to speak with him.

"Ava?" a deep, commanding voice broke through the silence.

"Yes. Is this Joe?"

"Call me Stone. Listen, I've tracked the data breach. Mostly."

She let out a breath, a mix of relief and determination. She knew time was running out, but she was driven to be the one to crack the case wide open. "So, what have you got?"

"As expected, it originated in China. I'm still piecing together the exact location, but all signs point to the government."

Typical. The Chinese government had a long history of hacking into U.S. systems. But why this bank? It wasn't prominent. It shouldn't have been on their radar.

"And the code?"

Stone paused. "First, we track the breach to identify who might have been expecting it. That'll give us clues to crack the code and where it's coming from."

The room fell silent as the implications sank in, each second intensifying the urgency.

That was sharp thinking. She hadn't even considered that angle. "Okay, I'll see what I can do, but I'm limited today." She knew her current setup wouldn't reveal more than he could find. She couldn't wait until tomorrow when her new equipment arrived.

She snapped her gaze to Grits with a quick thought. "What about the delivery guys? Won't they realize I'm here?"

Grits shook his head, both of them oblivious to the open phone call. "No, that's why I had you put everything in HIS's name. I'll handle the greeting. You stay hidden."

There's that bossy side again.

"Look, I'm a bit tired of—"

But Stone cut her off mid-sentence. "Guys?"

"What?" they both snapped into the phone, impatience clear.

"I've got a lot of work to do. Just checking in. Ava, did you have anything to share?"

She shook her head, then remembered he couldn't see her. "No, I just started working on the breach a couple of days ago. You're farther along than I was."

She'd lured her focus onto the code, instead of following a logical path. Regret washed over her. If only she'd never involved the authorities.

She wondered how the FBI would react when they followed up and found she was missing. Would they even look for her? Doubtful.

"Okay, then I'm off." He ended the call with a decisive click.

They exchanged a look. She shrugged one shoulder, silently acknowledging there was nothing more she could do for now. "What's the plan?"

He shrugged this time, a noncommittal move. "We wait for Daylan."

The name felt heavy in the air. Oh, yes. The man was supposed to help protect her. Yet, Grits didn't trust him one bit. Perfect. Neither did she.

CHAPTER TEN

"What do you mean you can't find them?" The man's voice cracked with rage, almost throwing his disposable cell across the room. He'd hired the best, or so he thought, but now he questioned their competence.

"They've gone off the grid."

He knew she was with HIS. So all he had to do was ask, and he'd have her location if it was shared. He already suspected the HIS agent had gone dark after the failed ambush at the safe house, and that thought made his fists clench. The incompetence stung worse than the failure itself.

These men had never failed him before, so he was confident that one waif of a woman shouldn't be a problem.

"She won't be able to resist. She'll be online soon. Then you can catch them."

"We'll try, but we hear she's super-smart with computers," came the reply.

And she was. That's how she'd uncovered the hidden code he'd concealed for the Chinese government inside the breach. No one looked in breaches for encrypted messages. They searched to find out who had triggered them.

The plan had worked flawlessly before. Now, he needed to relay troop movements to China, but he had no direct channel. Time was running out, and the stakes had never been higher.

He angrily paced in his office, lowering his voice so his staff assistants wouldn't catch his words. They were good at tuning out what was said behind closed doors, but he knew better than to take chances. Treason was something no one could ignore.

And, indeed, it was treason—plain and simple. The U.S. had put his son in harm's way, and now the country would pay the price. The government called it his son's "selfish sacrifice." But that was bullshit.

His son joined the military to earn money for college, not out of any sense of patriotic duty. Then, in the Navy, the SEALs called out to him. It took three tries, but he finally made it. His son had been so proud of that achievement.

Every day, a nightmare haunted him. The knowledge that his son was the first to be sent into dangerous, government-designated taboo spots.

Every time calls to his son went unanswered, he felt a gnawing sense of unease. As a member of the Senate Committee on Armed Services, he was confident he knew the ins and outs of every operation. If his son went dark, he'd pull every string, subpoena when necessary, to uncover the truth. His son was never out of reach—until that one fateful day. The call never came through.

They'd been ambushed en route to their target, and his son, along with two others, was killed. The remaining team was recalled, and a fresh team was dispatched to finish the mission, fully aware that everything had changed forever.

And now, everything was coming full circle.

Ava Sinclair, once an anomaly in his plans, had become the key to unlocking everything. The moment he learned she had called about a secure message—ears were everywhere—he knew she'd reach out to HIS team at some point, thanks to her friendship with Emily Hamilton. It'd taken a scare to get her to do it, but she had played it all perfectly.

He had already taken measures to keep the other HIS teams out of reach, leaving only one person left in the game—Rob Grimes, his son's team leader. The pieces were moving into place, and he relished the power of it all.

"Senator?" A sharp rap sounded on his door. He lowered his voice, indicating urgency to his hit team leader. "I'll call you back. I want better results, real soon." He ended the call abruptly, pocketing his phone with a sigh.

Sitting in his chair, he grabbed a handful of papers, trying to look busy as he spoke louder. "Come in."

A staff assistant stepped in, announcing, "Senator Hamilton is here to see you."

The man was a perennial pest, constantly dropping by under the guise of a visit when really, he just wanted to check on him. As the junior senator from Maryland, he was tied to this man. With a hint of disdain, he nodded. "Send him in."

He stood, walking around the desk with confidence, and extended his hand to the senior senator. "Blake, what can I do for you?"

Blake Hamilton grinned, his winning smile that had secured votes election after election. "Just checking in to see how everyone's doing."

He then returned behind his desk, letting out a light laugh, adding a touch of camaraderie to the meeting.

"You're checking in on me again, aren't you?"

Blake sighed. "You've got me. May I sit?"

Something was refreshing about this senator. He actually asked before assuming. Unlike other senior senators who just sat and expected him to cater to them, this man was different. The perfect man, even if his sons had hired the person responsible for his son's death. His gaze darkened as he thought about it. Yes, he blamed the team leader. After all, he had been the one to decide their final transport—the wrong transport.

"What's going on?" Blake's voice was sharp, his piercing gaze sweeping the room. "I'm concerned." He sank into one of the large leather chairs opposite his desk. "You're keeping my sons busy." He raised a hand to halt any protests. "Now, I usually like them to stay busy, but these last two contracts…it seems like the military should've handled them."

He paused, with a hint of a smirk curling at his lips. And, truth be told, they probably could have. If HIS's third team hadn't already been out on an operation, he might've found a contract for them, too. They'd wrapped up their mission early and returned. Still, sending them on vacation? That was his brilliant idea, planted in his mole's mind to keep things smooth.

Now that HIS had to rely on his mole to augment Ava's security, he'd soon uncover their exact location.

"They might have managed it, but your sons were perfectly positioned to help. Since the teams were already in the countries, I needed them there. Keeping us under the radar and preventing anyone from making another country entry."

"That makes sense, but keep an eye on the budget. You know how this time of year goes. The President's staff will start demanding numbers to plan next year's financials."

He nodded. His staff had already taken care of that. He went ahead and submitted it without checking with Blake, since Blake was not the committee chair.

"No worries. We're sitting pretty with plenty of funds to handle everything for the rest of this fiscal year." But in truth, the coffers were already running dry. When China makes moves, the U.S. military would be at a disadvantage, with limited funds to deploy its forces.

Blake studied him, and it unnerved him a bit. Despite his calm exterior, he knew his duplicity didn't show. No one would suspect he was tied to China. At least, not until they rewarded him after they took over most of the U.S.

To change the subject, he nodded toward Blake and asked, "How's married life?"

Blake smiled broadly. "Perfect. Elizabeth and I couldn't be happier."

Meanwhile, his own marriage had fallen apart after their only son was murdered. His wife couldn't handle his spiraling hostility, and he couldn't control his grief. That was the end of their marriage.

Blake stood up, a confident smile on his face. "How about we grab lunch later this week?"

He nodded in agreement. "That sounds great. I'll have

my staff sort it out."

Turning toward the door, Blake paused before adding, "Sounds good." Then, he turned back suddenly with a more serious look. "Did you hear that buzz about something in the last financial data breach?"

His eyes widened slightly as he appeared startled. "No? What exactly?"

Blake shrugged nonchalantly. "Some woman called the FTC—and it seems, the FBI—about an encrypted message she claimed was hidden in the code."

"Interesting. What are they doing about it?" He knew they weren't doing much because they thought she was a lunatic. It was all part of his plan, planting seeds of doubt.

"Nothing as far as I know, but I think they should."

He stayed silent, sensing what was coming next and trying to figure out how to avoid it.

"Listen, you're on the Committee for Commerce. Why don't you bring it up to the FTC head?"

He pretended to consider his words, then finally nodded. "I think that's a great idea."

He secretly plotted a counter-move. If Blake wanted the message checked into the system, he'd find someone else on the committee—perhaps the chair—to present it to the FTC. But he had to keep the FTC in the dark. It wasn't that he thought they could crack the code he and China had devised. It was a masterpiece, one that could have worked flawlessly—if only Ava Sinclair hadn't gotten involved. He'd eliminate her, even if she didn't decipher the code. Then, suddenly, a new idea sparked in his mind.

"Why don't we subpoena this woman? What was her name?"

Blake pondered for a moment. "Ava Sinclair."

The junior senator reached for his desk, as if grabbing a pen and paper. "Ava Sinclair, you said?" He jotted down the name, eyes still on Blake. "Do you know much about her?"

"I'll ask around."

"Great. Keep me posted, and we'll get her in here to tell her side."

Blake nodded slowly. "That's wise." Then, hesitating slightly, he added, "But there's a problem. The FBI checked on her, and she's vanished."

He acted stunned, his eyes widening with concern. "Do you really think she's okay? Maybe she's just on vacation or hiding out somewhere."

Blake shook his head firmly. "No, she's gone."

"That certainly makes things more complicated."

The tension between them was palpable.

Blake nodded, his expression grim. "Yeah, so, tread carefully with this one."

He watched in silence as Blake turned sharply and disappeared from his office. A nagging doubt crept into his mind. Was the warning just about watching out for his safety, or was there more beneath the surface? Suspicion grew. Did Blake somehow suspect him? He pushed the thought aside and decided to add another name to his list of enemies. The target was more challenging now, guarded by the Secret Service due to his position as party leader, especially after his wife had been kidnapped before. But he was undeterred. There was always a way.

Smirking slightly, he casually pulled his phone from his pocket. "I've got another job for you."

CHAPTER ELEVEN

Ava was seconds away from tossing her laptop out the window. It was painfully slow and wouldn't run the software she needed for cybersecurity work. Basically, all it could do was check email, which she avoided like the plague, knowing she could be traced if she clicked the wrong link.

Frustrated, she shoved the laptop aside and wondered why she even kept it. Nostalgia maybe? It was her first major purchase after college, unplanned for running a business, so she hadn't thought it through. It was one of those Black Friday deals she simply couldn't resist.

Grits stepped in from what he called "rounds," a term she was familiar with but found amusing when he tried to explain it. She'd seen enough television to know what was happening and had mixed feelings about her current life.

As he passed by, he nodded silently and headed toward his bedroom. When he returned, he carried a small arsenal of weapons. Carefully, he laid each one out on a towel at the table, and she watched in silence as he meticulously disassembled and cleaned each firearm.

Throughout the process, his silence was deafening. He

was deliberately avoiding conversation, lost in his own world of routine and ritual.

She cleared her throat, breaking the silence. "I'll whip up something for lunch." She stood, eager for his response, but all she received was a simple nod.

In the pantry, she spotted a box of pasta salad that just needed boiling and a spoonful of mayonnaise. Not a culinary masterpiece, but she could handle that, and she loved this pasta. After preparing the meal and adding some canned fruit on the side for a sweet touch, she carried it to the now-empty table and set it down with a sense of quiet satisfaction.

By the time lunch was ready, Grits was perched on the edge of the couch, elbows resting on his knees, his gaze fixed on the cold fireplace as if it held the answers he couldn't find.

Ava stood a few feet away, arms crossed, still tasting him on her lips and feeling the sting of the ache it left behind. The silence between them grew heavy until she finally broke it. "You're avoiding me."

Grits didn't turn around. His voice was steady but guarded. "I'm protecting you."

Her lips parted, a response lingering on her tongue, but she couldn't help but think, "That's not what that kiss felt like."

He exhaled slowly, his breath ragged with emotion. "That kiss was a mistake."

She inhaled sharply, the words hitting her harder than any bullet. Her eyes widened, jaw tightening in disbelief. "Wow. You didn't seem to think so at the time."

He stood rapidly, almost impatiently—like being still

was too much to bear—and faced her squarely. "You don't think I want this?" His voice was rough, trembling with raw emotion. "You think I haven't been trying like hell not to touch you since we met?"

Her heart pounded. "Then why—"

"Because there's a line, Ava. A line I absolutely won't cross. You're a client. My job is to protect you, and I won't risk losing you over some stupid mistake because I was more interested in you than my surroundings."

Her eyes shimmered with emotion. "You don't get to make that choice for me, Grits. I've been hunted, shot at, and you're the only person who's made me feel safe. I need real. I need you."

He took a shaky breath, heart pounding. "And if I let myself need you back?"

"Then maybe—" she stepped into him, her hand resting gently on his chest, "—we both should stop pretending this isn't real."

His hands hovered at her waist, hesitant, as if she were fragile glass.

Just as tension reached its peak, a sudden noise from the drive shattered the moment. They froze, turning in unison.

They broke apart as if caught in the act, tension crackling in the air.

He cleared his throat, voice steady but tense. "Daylan's here."

Ava's heart pounded, but in a different way. She hoped he hadn't seen them together like that. The stakes had never felt higher. She'd already crossed a line with Grits. She wouldn't get him in trouble for "crossing that line."

"I'd best go out and meet him. You stay here."

She bristled at that. She needed fresh air. "Since he's safe, I want to come with you." To avoid coming across as pushy, she added, "I could really use some fresh air."

The gentle look he gave her melted her heart. He had so many scars that kept him from enjoying their time together. Granted, it'd only been a day, but still, it seemed like forever.

"Okay, but you listen to what I tell you to do."

She smiled and nodded. Yes, a bit of freedom.

She ran her fingers through her hair, her heart fluttering with a mix of nerves and anticipation. She hoped she looked presentable, not for royalty this time, but for someone just as important—an employee who might not even realize how much he mattered.

As they stepped out and descended the stairs, the quiet hum of the afternoon was broken by Daylan releasing a large German Shepherd from the back of his SUV. The dog's excited bark signaled the end of any time she and Grits would have alone.

The dog was stunning, its coat shimmering in the sunlight. She felt a tug to rush over and pet it, but a cautious voice in her head held her back. Dogs could be unpredictable, even when with a handler. Especially if they were in what she could only call a "protect mode."

As she watched, a tall, blond-haired man approached the vehicle. He paused in front of them, nodding to the man beside her. "Grits." Then he turned, his face alight with a warm, inviting smile, to her. "You must be Ava."

She couldn't help but smile back, a warmth spreading

through her as she extended her hand with a friendly gesture. "It's nice to meet you, Daylan." After a brief handshake that made Grits growl softly, she turned to his K9 companion. "What's his name?"

Daylan's face brightened. "Buddy." Pride radiated from him as he looked down at his dog, clearly proud of his furry friend. "Buddy, Gib Laut."

Buddy barked loudly, his tail wagging excitedly. Daylan shrugged. "That's just his way of saying 'Hello.'"

The moment was simple, yet full of unspoken warmth and friendship.

Daylan startled, a flicker of surprise crossing his face. "Oh, Ava, I've got something for you."

She instinctively caught Grits' tense posture beside her, sensing his unease. Was he worried that this man might be a threat? Grits had said he didn't trust him. So why? Despite the suspicion, Daylan appeared harmless enough as he strode to the back of his SUV and opened it.

"Devon mentioned you might want this, since Emily said you wouldn't want to wait for your own."

Ava's cheeks flushed with embarrassment. Em knew she had little patience, and now both men did too. She didn't like her vulnerabilities on display, yet she understood that perhaps Em's instincts weren't meant to be hurtful.

Daylan returned, carrying a sleek laptop bag, and Ava's heart almost leapt into her throat. She swiftly snatched it, holding it close to her chest as if it were a precious secret. "Yes." Devon would know precisely what she needed to solve this puzzle.

Daylan hesitated, confusion flickering across his face.

"Devon said it should do the trick for now." He shook his head. "But I'm not quite sure what 'now' means."

Grits stepped forward with a determined look. "She ordered equipment to arrive tomorrow, but this—" he gestured to the laptop bag "—will help us get moving right away."

Ava's eyes sparkled with anticipation as she turned to Grits, who nodded encouragingly. Heart pounding, she nearly sprinted back up the cabin steps, eager to see what Devon had sent. Once she sank into the seat Grits had earlier guided her to—still haunted by the memory of that unforgettable kiss—she unzipped the bag with a sense of purpose. Inside, she revealed her laptop, mouse, and thumb drives, all tools she'd need. She rubbed her hands together, a determined smile spreading across her face. She was in business, and nothing was going to stop her now.

* * * *

Grits watched Ava race back into the cabin, a swirl of longing in his chest he desperately hoped wouldn't betray him. As she disappeared inside, he shifted his gaze to Daylan, a twinge of frustration brewing. Why did it have to be Daylan? With a resigned sigh, he decided to be transparent. "Listen, I don't trust you, but you're here. If you double-cross us, I'll kill you myself."

Daylan's eyes widened in surprise. He quickly raised his hands, signaling for silence before Grits could speak again. "Listen, man, I regret outing Pup and Elena. It was a mistake, I admit that. But back then, I genuinely believed he was risking her life by crossing that line."

The infernal line seemed to haunt him, especially during his time with Ava. Perhaps, he thought, once she was safe....

"But I've been doing my best to earn everyone's trust back."

Grits grunted, unimpressed. He hadn't seen anything the man had done that deserved redemption. He bared watching.

"Well, this is your big chance to prove yourself and earn my trust. I need you to help me keep her safe—no matter what."

Daylan nodded, determination flashing in his eyes. "Whatever Buddy and I can do, we'll do it."

He assessed the agent, then continued, "There's another room. It only has a double bed, but that should be enough for you and Buddy. Rest up. Things are about to get complicated."

"Hey, I almost forgot." Daylan turned back toward the SUV.

Grits followed curiously.

"Emily did some shopping while I packed up my gear. That's why I'm so late."

Grits' eyes lit up at the sight of the groceries: fresh milk, ripe fruit, and more.

Bless Emily. Grits grabbed the plastic bags to take to the cabin and stash in the refrigerator. Meanwhile, Daylan hoisted his duffel, a small bag of dog food, and weapons, and with Buddy trotting behind, they headed toward the cabin.

"I heard about the challenges you've faced."

Grits turned fast, and Daylan must've caught his flash

of suspicion. Jesse may trust him, but Grits still didn't. He'd plan an evac from this location and their next steps in case of trouble. And Daylan might be that trouble.

"Jesse filled me in."

Grits' voice was low and serious. "You're not to share anything with anyone. Not even your team leader."

Daylan shrugged nonchalantly. "Justin is on vacation, so I wouldn't bother him anyway."

Grits almost forgot that the Charlie team leader was Justin Franks, Ballpark's brother. He realized he needed to get to know him better. The Alpha and Bravo teams were so close because they'd once been one team. They hadn't truly embraced Charlie team, and Grits was determined to change that once he returned.

When they stepped into the cabin, Ava was utterly absorbed in her computer, her gaze never leaving the screen. He grimaced, knowing she needed to be more aware of her surroundings. He made a mental note to discuss it with her later.

Daylan whistled softly, a mischievous grin on his face. "Boy, she's really into it, isn't she?"

Grits nodded, heading toward the refrigerator with purpose. "Fingers crossed she can crack this thing so we can get her home safe and sound."

Daylan chuckled and smiled mischievously. "Yeah, so she and Em can do more shopping."

Grits beamed as he finished stacking the cold groceries in the fridge. "I hear they nearly cleaned out a bookstore in just a weekend." He looked for a reaction, but when nothing came, he shrugged, a little bemused.

Daylan settled at the table, spooning a mouthful of

pasta. After a tentative taste, he glanced at Grits, waiting for approval.

They ate in comfortable silence until finally, Daylan leaned back with a satisfied sigh and rubbed his belly. "I've got a plan for you."

Something about the way Daylan said that made Grits know he couldn't trust that plan one bit. He silently cursed. Why had Jesse sent the enemy to their safe haven?

CHAPTER TWELVE

Grits stood outside the cabin, his eyes fixed on Daylan as the agent watched Ava work. Despite the urge to scan the perimeter for threats, he couldn't shake the feeling that Daylan was their leak. He wondered what had warped Jesse's trust in him.

Frustration clenched in his gut as he realized their situation was precarious. They had to move, leave this cabin without Daylan, and do it soon. His gut told him their time here was running out. Where would they go next?

He rubbed his hand over his five o'clock shadow, glancing over the landscape one last time. It was almost time to switch out with Daylan. And honestly, he couldn't wait for that moment—anything to get Daylan away from Ava.

Daylan's relentless flirtations had her laughing and flashing smiles, even returning a flirtatious glimmer or two. The memory of it all made him growl in frustration, desire, and possessiveness.

He trudged to the front of the cabin, every step heavy with urgency, and froze when he heard Ava's soft, melodic laughter. Time was running out. Tomorrow, they would have to move at dawn. Amidst the mounting danger, he had one unwavering friend he could rely on. Though the thought of bringing him into this peril made his stomach churn. Still, it was a risk he had to take.

Grits hurried up the stairs two at a time, eager to reach the house and intervene. As he peeked inside, his eyes landed on Daylan, leaning casually over the kitchen bar, his face lit up with a bright smile, and Ava's laughter rang through the room. He looked so relaxed, so genuine—too genuine.

Grits' heart skipped a beat, and jealousy gnawed at his gut. Was Daylan really just chatting, or was there something more to it? Was Daylan trying to pull secrets from her, testing whether she could decode the message? With her minor in cryptology, Grits knew her skills weren't just a hobby—they were a hidden weapon. And that thought sent a shiver down his spine.

Yanking open the door with a burst of energy, Grits strode into the room, eyes scanning sharply. He fixed Daylan with a pointed gaze. "Your turn."

Daylan nodded calmly, then turned to Ava with a warm smile. "It was really nice chatting with you, Ava."

She returned the smile, her eyes bright. "Likewise."

"Buddy, hier."

The dog, resting by the cold fireplace, got up and trotted to Daylan.

As Daylan and his K9 prepared to leave, he paused, eyes locking on Grits. "Take care of her."

Grits' brow furrowed in anger. "What's that supposed to mean?" he growled, tension tightening his voice.

Without looking back, Daylan simply laughed softly

and waved over his shoulder. "You'll figure it out."

Watching Daylan leave, Grits couldn't shake the uneasy feeling gnawing at him that their time here was up. Tonight, Ava would stay by his side. Come dawn, they would set out—without Daylan and his K9.

"That was rude."

Grits turned to see Ava casually placing a glass in the dishwasher.

"What?"

"I said that was rude."

His eyes narrowed. "What was?"

"Your growling at him." Her tone was edged with irritation.

Grits' brow furrowed at her tone. Yet, he kept his suspicions close, knowing the truth was better kept quiet for now. "I'm starving. Let me whip up some dinner." He headed to the kitchen.

"Oh, Daylan beat you to it." Ava smiled. "There's stir-fried chicken and fried rice on the stove."

As he approached, he couldn't shake the feeling that everything was too perfect. Had Daylan spent the time cooking, prying information from Ava?

An uneasy itch crept into his mind. Maybe they should leave now. Something wasn't quite right, and his instincts screamed at him to pay attention.

Passing Ava by the stove, he inhaled her fragrant scent, his senses awash with longing. Desire surged, but the fear of endangering her kept him restrained. Grabbing a plate and loading it with the food he hoped hadn't been poisoned by Daylan, he took a seat at the bar beside Ava, who was now immersed in her computer work once again.

"Any luck with the message?"

She shook her head and let out a sigh. "No. It's tough encryption, really tricky stuff."

"Do you need the stuff you ordered, or is this enough?"

They wouldn't be there to accept delivery. He planned to repay her for the equipment. Well, he'd reimburse HIS since she hadn't actually paid for it yet.

"I'd prefer what I ordered, but this will do." She had a determined look in her eyes. "I've got the best software downloaded to decrypt the message, but it's in a code I've never seen before. I haven't been active as a cryptologist recently, so it's all pretty unfamiliar to me."

He hoped Stone was having better luck because they desperately needed to figure out who was after Ava and put an end to it.

"Maybe Stone is having some luck." He tried to lift her spirits.

But she just sighed, her shoulders slumping.

Somehow, he suspected Devon was itching to crack the code himself. Yet, if the doctor and Rylee didn't want him to have a computer, he'd follow their orders. Grits still couldn't believe Devon had suffered a heart attack. It was mild, but a heart attack was a heart attack, and it reminded him how fragile life could be.

After finishing his meal, he cleared his plate and placed it in the dishwasher. He grabbed a bottle of water from the refrigerator, then leaned back at the bar, eyes fixed on Ava. She was mesmerizing. Her intense stare at the computer sent a shiver straight to his gut. He was utterly hooked, and deep down, he knew it. If only he could hold himself back until she was safe, then maybe they could see if there was more than just a fiery attraction between them.

He sensed she wanted more based on her passionate speech after the kiss. However, it was a mistake. Not the kiss itself, but the timing. With killers closing in on them, pursuing an affair wasn't just reckless—it was dangerous. Still, the pull was strong, and he wondered how long he could resist.

She didn't look up from her laptop. "You're staring at me."

Caught in the act, he didn't bother to hide his gaze. He grinned. "I was."

Finally, she shifted her gaze, eyes narrowing playfully. "And?"

He let out a gentle sigh. "And, after this is over, we're going on a date."

Ava raised her eyebrows, a teasing smile creeping onto her lips. "Oh, we are? Are we now?"

He nodded confidently, a grin spreading across his face. "We are."

The tension dissolved into shared laughter, their connection undeniable.

She tilted her head, a playful challenge in her eyes. "Does this mean the kiss wasn't a mistake?"

He hesitated, then flashed her a bittersweet smile. "No. It was."

She opened her mouth to argue, but he cut her off, his tone gentle yet firm.

"The wrong time. Not wrong."

"Oh." She paused, her expression softly contemplative. "The line."

He nodded, a knowing smile touching his lips. "The line. It's there for a reason." The weight of unspoken feelings hung in the space between them like a thundercloud.

Finally, she shrugged. "Okay."

He blinked, surprised she didn't seem more affected, and found himself momentarily speechless.

She looked out the window, then back at him. "So, what's next?"

He noticed she wasn't upset about the "line." "We're leaving in the morning."

She paused, then grinned. "The three of us. Well, and the dog."

He shook his head, a small smile forming. "Just you and me. And I expect you to keep that to yourself."

Tension lingered thick in the air.

"But Daylan—" she began, her voice tinged with pleading.

"No Daylan."

"But why? Didn't you say you needed the extra help?"

They did need help, but they'd get it from someone he trusted implicitly—Brian Zelter. The old NCO, a recluse by nature, was a genius with computers and security. His place? Entirely impenetrable, a fortress built on expertise.

"We're going to have help." He hoped one of the HIS teams would return soon for backup. Until then, he knew he could count on his old Navy SEAL contacts. Those that no one at the agency knew.

"Who?"

"Brian Zelter. Old friend of mine." He smiled, thinking of Brian and the times they'd spent together in and out of the zone.

"From your time as a SEAL?"

He froze for a moment, the question catching him off guard. He hadn't recalled revealing that detail. "How did you know that?"

She shrugged, a slight smile playing on her lips. "Daylan mentioned it."

He leaned in slightly. "What else did he say?"

She closed her laptop, turning fully to face him, her eyes glinting with a hint of amusement. "He's really into his job at HIS, but he messed up early on. Now, no one's giving him a break. I'm practically his golden ticket to show that he's one of you."

So, Daylan was sweet-talking his way into her good graces, trying to butter her up. Well, that ship will set sail come morning.

She hesitated, concern flickering across her face. "How are we supposed to leave without him noticing?"

Grits took a slow sip of water, then exhaled deeply. "We'll do it after the shift change. When he's out cold." He stood and cleared his throat. "Let me call Brian and warn him we're coming."

"You don't feel bad bringing this danger to his doorstep?"

He shook his head, a grim resolve in his eyes. "Right now, there's nowhere else I'd rather be."

As he turned to walk away, he pulled out the cell HIS had given him for this operation. It was supposed to be untraceable, but he knew better—nothing was truly anonymous these days. He keyed in the number from memory and waited for the line to come alive. Glancing toward the front of the cabin, he saw Daylan and Buddy patrolling the perimeter. At least he was pretending to care.

When the line finally answered, an awkward silence hung in the air. Knowing Brian wasn't about to speak to someone he didn't know, Grits decided to break the ice first. "Salty, it's Grits."

A low chuckle came from the other end of the line. "Grits, what's wrong?"

"Why does everything have to be wrong for me to call an old buddy?"

There was a brief pause before Salty replied, "No one just calls me, you know. What's going on?"

Grits felt a pang of sympathy for the recluse, but he understood this was how the man had chosen to live after leaving the SEALs. "Okay, I need your help."

"What exactly?"

"Is your place still secure?"

The recluse's voice hardened with pride. "I've got the best security and traps available. No one gets in without a fight."

"Good, because we're bringing a fight straight to your door." With a determined smile, Grits exchanged details, then he ended the call and turned to Ava, who sat watching him intently. "He'll be ready for us."

"And what about tonight?"

"You're sleeping with me tonight. No arguments."

CHAPTER THIRTEEN

Ava's eyes widened in surprise at the statement. "But you just said—"

Grits cut her off with a grin. "I didn't mean sex. I meant sleep. You'll sleep in my bed. Nothing more."

She tilted her head, smiling. "Are you sure about that?"

He narrowed his eyes, a hint of amusement flickering in his gaze.

She giggled mischievously. "Just checking that line."

Grits shook his head, chuckling softly.

It was good to have some levity amid their heavy conversations. She was still on the run, deeper into the mystery, without a clue more than when they started. Clearly, she needed a real cryptologist because her skills were minimal at best.

Looking back at the closed laptop, she shook her head with a sigh. "My eyes need a break from the screen."

"What about watching a movie?"

She shook her head again, a faint smile on her lips. "No, it's still a screen. I think I'll go pack."

Grits hesitated, then started to speak, his tone cautious. "About that—" he began, and she knew she wouldn't like what he was about to say. "We travel light. No big suitcases to lug around. It's too risky for Daylan to hear us."

"But—" she started, and he raised his hand to stop her.

"Just the shoulder and the laptop bag. Only what you can carry—no rolling suitcases."

She understood his reasoning, but she still couldn't wrap her mind around not trusting Daylan. He wasn't the leak Grits believed him to be. In fact, he was actually trying to find the real leak himself, to prove his innocence in Grits' eyes.

"Also," he added as she was walking away, "wear to bed what you'll wear in the morning."

She turned back to him, brows raised in surprise. "Shoes and all?"

He paused, then shook his head with a slight smile. "I think we can do without them."

Thank goodness. She had a hard time sleeping with socks on or feet tucked under the covers.

She headed to her assigned bedroom and began packing her shoulder bag. It only held two days' worth of clothes, rolled tightly, but she stuffed in plenty of underwear—definitely not wearing the same pair two days in a row. The bra? She'd survive, but underwear? Eww.

She grabbed her deodorant, brush, face moisturizer, toothbrush, and toothpaste, stuffing them into her bag with hurried precision. Today, she was willing to trade a day of luxury for safety. At the last second, her hand paused over her travel bottle of perfume. She wasn't sure she'd wear it, but something instinctive told her to take it along.

Sitting on the bed's edge, she pondered her dilemma. Grits' insistence on extra protection sent a cold shiver down her spine. She knew she was in real danger. Yet, when immersed in her computer code, her worries faded into nothingness—just lines of logic and purpose. That feeling of focus was strangely reassuring, especially amid her current predicament.

Glancing at her now-dead smartwatch, she hurriedly grabbed her chargers and tossed them into her bag. As she slipped out of her room, her eyes caught Grits waiting just outside the door. Her heart skittered with a rush of adrenaline. "What?" Had something already happened? Were they on the move? The tension in the air was palpable.

"I was just about to grab your bag and stash it in my room while Daylan was out back."

"Oh." She reached into her room, grabbed the bag, and handed it to him. "Thanks."

She followed him to his room, eyes widening at the sight of the king-sized bed. Celeb clearly prioritized comfort even while camping. The spacious bed allowed them to sleep apart without touching. It was a detail that brought a twinge of sadness to her.

Grits cleared his throat, his voice steady yet filled with an unspoken determination. "If you don't mind, I'd like to sleep closest to the door."

She nodded, understanding his silent promise to shield her from whatever danger might lurk beyond the door. An unexpected ache tightened in her chest, a bittersweet pain brought on by knowing he was willing to risk himself for her sake.

After she toed off her shoes, she crawled across the bed, pressing herself against the wall. The sensation of being both trapped and safe was a strange paradox, yet with Grits by her side, she felt an inexplicable comfort.

Grits settled on the edge of the bed, methodically removing his earpiece, then weapon, extra clip, and placing them on the nightstand. His movements were deliberate, revealing a hidden knife sheathed at his side, which he discreetly tucked under his pillow.

In that moment, she realized he was not just ready to protect her. He was prepared to fight for her safety with unwavering resolve.

After a tense ten minutes of lying on their backs, careful not to even let their hands touch, Grits boldly placed his open palm in the space between them.

Though she knew she shouldn't jump to conclusions, she did, relishing the thought. With a gentle motion, she slid her hand into his.

He held it firmly, squeezing with determination. "I'm going to see you through this, Ava."

She smiled, knowing he believed he could handle it alone, and she trusted him completely. "I know."

"Then, date."

She nodded, her eyes tracing the ceiling. "A date."

He turned to her. "Where would you like to go?"

She turned to him, meeting his gaze. "Probably somewhere to eat. Just not seafood."

His expression was almost comical, a mix of shock and dismay. "You don't like seafood?"

"Oh, I do," she assured him. "Just not for a first date.

Crabs are too messy, and everything else leaves a lingering smell."

He burst into laughter. "Thank God, because if you didn't like seafood, we'd be in trouble."

She giggled. "Are you a big seafood fan?"

He grinned widely. "The biggest."

"We'll be just fine, but let's keep it balanced."

Grits released her hand and propped himself up on his side, curiosity in his eyes. "What drove you to leave the government and venture out on your own?"

She playfully matched his pose, resting her head on the pillow. "And what prompted you to trade in your SEALs gear for the private sector?"

He chuckled, a hint of admiration in his voice. "Touché."

"How about we save that for our first date?"

"First implies there will be more."

She smiled. "At least three, because I never sleep with a guy before the third date."

He leaned in, his finger gently tracing her jawline, sending delightful shivers of anticipation down her spine. "Three, huh?"

"Yeah." Her smile widened. "It's a line." Then she giggled.

His laughter was like a melody that danced right into her heart. A man so dedicated to safeguarding others deserved a sprinkle of joy in his life, and she was determined to be the one to provide it for Grits. Speaking of which—

"I don't even know your real name."

His laughter faded, but a warm smile lingered. "Rob

Grimes."

"Robert?"

"Yes, but I don't prefer it."

"All right, Rob." She tested the name on her lips before raising an eyebrow. "I must admit, I prefer Grits."

He grinned. "That's been my nickname since my SEAL days."

"Why Grits?"

He chuckled, shaking his head. "I couldn't fathom why they didn't include grits in our MREs. Sure, instant wasn't ideal, but it was manageable. The guys found that hilarious."

"Your guys?"

He paused, considering his words. "Isn't that a bit of a second-date conversation?"

She laughed, charmed by his playful response. "Oh, so there are different levels of conversation, huh?" Despite his rugged exterior, this man was undeniably endearing.

He gently tucked a strand of her hair behind her ear, his voice soft yet commanding. "Ava."

Her breath caught, her heart tripping over itself at the intensity in his tone. "Yes?"

"I'm going to kiss you now." His eyes locked on her.

"I thought it wasn't advisable."

He shook his head, closing the distance between them with deliberate slowness. "It's not."

"The line."

"Damn the line."

Then his mouth claimed hers, tender and soft, yet edged with a gentle urgency that shattered her defenses, leaving her momentarily breathless. His lips moved over hers with a fervent need, more persuasive than she was willing to admit, igniting a forbidden need that she had tried to suppress. His tongue traced the delicate fullness of her lips with a teasing precision, eliciting shivers of delight that coursed through her body like a warm wave. Seizing the moment, she parted her lips in silent invitation, allowing him to enter, and reciprocated with a hunger that burned fiercely inside.

Grits closed the small, intimate distance between them, her body instinctively turning slightly to better access his lips as he leaned in. This was exactly what she wanted—a distraction from the storm raging around her life. But beneath that desire, she knew deep down that Grits wasn't just a fleeting distraction. This had the potential to be something genuine. Still, she couldn't help but wonder—did things built on such urgent, impulsive moments ever truly end well?

His lips left hers abruptly. "Quit thinking and just kiss me."

How had he known her mind was gently drifting away, caught in a whirl of doubt and hesitation?

His demanding lips returned to hers, possessively and confidently caressing in a way that magically cleared her thoughts, erasing all doubts and worries, leaving only this present moment…the heat of his touch…the rhythm of their breathing…and the overwhelming feeling of connection building between them.

It was in that moment, however, that she recalled he'd broken the line for her. That pause in thought made her lips still, caught between desire and hesitation.

With a reluctant groan, Grits reluctantly pulled his lips

away from hers. "What?"

"Are you really sure about crossing this line? I don't want to be something you regret later."

In the soft glow of the en-suite bathroom light, which he had thoughtfully left on to guide her through the night, Grits' eyes locked onto hers.

"Don't worry. I won't regret it later. I can promise you that, Ava."

Just hearing him say her name sent a shiver of delight down her spine. She had an intense desire, no, a deep craving, for another kiss. "Then, kiss me again."

"You don't have to tell me twice."

His lips pressed urgently against hers before she had the chance to inhale for her next breath, leaving her momentarily breathless. This time, their kiss was more intense, harder, more demanding, and insistent, causing her to gasp sharply at the sudden surge of emotion and anticipation coursing through her. The kiss was a searing, soldering heat that radiated through her entire body, sending shockwaves of raw, burning lust deep into her core. It ignited a fiery passion that refused to be contained, spreading warmth and intensity throughout her being, as if every nerve ending was alive with the electric sensation.

Buddy barked, and gunfire erupted.

CHAPTER FOURTEEN

Adrenaline surged through Grits as he grabbed Ava and rolled her off the bed in a loud thump. "Stay down!" he barked, already grabbing his weapon, extra clip, and earpiece from the nightstand, then crawling to the bathroom and flicking the lights off. He returned and crouched beside her, his breath harsh and steady.

"Are you okay?" They had hit the floor on their side, hard, when they'd rolled, and he worried she might've been injured.

"No. Someone is shooting at us."

In the suffocating darkness of the room, he couldn't make out her eyes, but he was certain fear lurked there, as it had been reflected in the tremors that wracked her body as he had rolled her off the bed.

His movements were careful as he covered Ava. He pushed the blinds aside, peering out the window with anticipation. The scene out back was clear.

Her voice broke through the silence. "How did they find us?"

"I don't know."

He pressed his earpiece in and called "Sitrep" as he put on his shoes.

Daylan's voice crackled in his ear. "Two shooters. They're damn drones." That meant someone, or someones, was close enough to control them. There was no way he was leaving Ava alone to handle those drones. But depending on their size, they could be carrying a hefty load of ammunition.

"Can you handle it?"

"Sure—"

More gunfire erupted, followed by an eerie silence, heavy with anticipation.

"Daylan?" Grits called out urgently.

"I'm hit."

Should he help Daylan or rush back to protect Ava? In that brief moment of indecision, he knew one thing: he had to find out what was happening now.

A flicker of doubt crossed his face, but urgency pushed him forward. "Stay here." Without waiting for a response, he moved swiftly, his heart pounding fiercely. He threw open the bedroom door and shut it with resolve. He needed to understand the threat. Was it a lone wolf or were they in for a group of mercenaries?

Staying in the shadows, he moved toward the front of the house where sporadic gunfire still rang out. The front glass shattered violently, and he scrambled behind the sofa, seeking cover. It wasn't the sturdiest shield, but it was enough to hide him from view.

Peering out, he spotted Daylan sprawled on the front steps, nearly motionless. Only his gun arm was active, holding his weapon as he fired until the chamber was empty. Buddy lay at his side, barking.

Grits knew this was his moment. It was now or never.

With a burst of adrenaline, he lunged from his hiding spot, racing toward Daylan to destroy the deadly drones and drag Daylan to safety, no matter what.

"I've got your six," Grits informed the downed agent.

"Get her the fuck out of here. I've got this!"

Grits spotted one of the large white drones zip by and instinctively pulled the trigger. "Like hell you do." He unleashed a flurry of shots that finally sent the drone tumbling to the ground, lifeless. His eyes darted around, searching for the second drone. Spotting it about twenty yards away, he took careful aim and fired again. He emptied his clip, then quickly reloaded, adrenaline coursing through him. The remaining drone kept firing wildly, a frantic burst of sparks and noise. It was either a novice controller or one desperate to do as much damage as possible before the enemy arrived.

Unable to move to help the other agent, he watched helplessly as Daylan bled on the steps, a surge of rage igniting within him. If Daylan had been in on this, that would have been a shitty way to repay him for sharing their location. Then, a cold realization hit that he'd probably been wrong about Daylan all along. But someone had leaked their position, and only he, Jesse, Celeb, and Daylan knew it. That was too many mouths.

He aimed at the drone again, his shot true this time, smashing it sideways. As it circled back, he sprinted to Daylan, hoping Buddy didn't bite him, grabbed the collar of Daylan's shirt, and yanked him free from danger.

Before he could gauge the severity of the other agent's injuries, the drone unleashed another barrage of gunfire through the cabin, destroying Celeb's beautiful getaway and throwing glass everywhere. A shard or two brushed his cheek, but he didn't flinch.

His heart pounding fiercely in his chest, he sprang to his feet just as the gunfire rained around him. Without hesitation, he aimed again at the relentless drone. It had to be running out of ammunition soon—serving only as a distraction while the actual threat, whoever was behind this chaos, closed in.

Tension thickened in the air, and he prepared for what was coming next.

A pickup truck roared toward them, and Grits' heart nearly stopped. Panic surged as he realized he had to reach Ava. The truck screeched to a halt with a deafening skid. The driver flung open the door, and someone fired. Unable to see through the blinding headlights, it took a moment to realize the driver wasn't shooting at him but at the drone that soared overhead. Within seconds, the drone plummeted to the ground, lifeless.

"Is it clear?" a voice called out from the truck.

Grits couldn't suppress a grin as a rush of adrenaline surged through him. Salty had never waited around. He'd always arrived just in the nick of time. "Clear the area!" he commanded, voice booming to his old teammate. "I've got wounded."

Daylan's grip on his shirt was tight as he reached out desperately. "Get Ava the fuck out of here."

Her name hit him like a lightning bolt. Ava! His heart pounded with urgency. He yearned to check on her, but first, Daylan needed help. "Salty! I need you in here!"

In seconds, the solid man charged up the stairs, sidestepping the blood pooling beneath Daylan. "Shit, boss. You pissed off someone with skills." His grim chuckle echoed in the room along with Buddy's growl.

Daylan said something to the dog he didn't understand, and Buddy calmed and lay beside Daylan, head on Daylan's legs.

Grits nodded, trusting him. "Help him. I've got to check on Ava." Heart pounding, he sprinted to the bedroom, flung the door open, and was blindsided by a flying book. He stumbled back, blinking. "Ava!"

Her trembling hands reached out to touch his bleeding cheek. "Oh my God, Grits. I'm so sorry." Her eyes were wide with fear. "I thought you—were—" Her voice cracked, and he saw her about to break down. He pulled her into his arms, determined to keep her safe, no matter what.

Knowing they had no time to waste, Grits urgently pushed Ava aside and snatched his cell phone. "Grab your bags. We're leaving."

Concern was etched on her face. "What about Daylan and Buddy?"

"Grab your bags, Ava." He hesitated for a moment, choosing not to reveal that Daylan was injured, fearing she might rush to help and jeopardize their escape.

She nodded swiftly and turned to gather her belongings. Grits noticed Ava had already slipped on her shoes. Good girl. They needed to move quickly. They'd be traveling light, fast, and ready for anything.

Returning to the living room, Ava's eyes immediately locked onto Salty, and she came to a halt, her steps momentarily frozen. Grits recognized that Salty looked downright intimidating with his burly physique and full tattoos sprawling across his arms.

The tension in the room thickened.

"It's okay. It's my buddy, Salty."

She nodded, but her reaction was hesitant, her feet rooted to the spot. That was, until her gaze shifted downward, revealing Daylan on the ground. Without hesitation, she dropped her bags and fell to her knees beside him. "Daylan!"

Buddy whined softly, and Ava instinctively reached out to pet the loyal K9. It was remarkable. Whatever command Buddy had been given, it allowed him to shift focus immediately and tend to his master, a true testament to the bond they shared.

Salty quickly stood and moved closer to him, his tone sharp with concern. "It's not good, boss."

"I can call Life Flight right now for him." He went to dial on his phone.

"Why don't you make the call from my truck while you two hurry up and get out of here before those bad guys arrive? I can handle this. Meet you at Nick's Café."

Grits nodded, knowing the place well. It was near Salty's home, a spot he'd been special enough to visit only once before.

"How will you get there?"

"Don't worry about me. I'll be there before daylight."

Grits understood the old promise between buddies. Salty would fight his way out if he had to and still be there before sunrise. "Don't shoot at my guys when they arrive."

Salty winked. "Only the bad guys."

"How'd you find us?" He knew he hadn't disclosed

his location to Salty, but the man had mad skills.

"Two ways." A sly grin crept on his face. "I traced that untraceable phone since we stayed on the line so long." He gestured toward the front of the cabin. "And the GPS in that thing."

"But my SUV was turned off."

Salty shook his head, a glint of confidence in his eyes. "Doesn't matter on some vehicles. Now, git."

Grits hesitated, reluctant to leave Salty alone, knowing someone would come after them, along with the expensive drones to cover their tracks. But he couldn't risk Ava being here either. Grabbing her arm, he urged, "We have to go."

"But, Daylan." Her eyes brimmed with tears, and his heart pounded in his chest at the sight.

"He's going to be fine. Let's go."

Daylan reached out instinctively, his voice barely above a whisper. "Get out of here, Ava."

She hesitated, then nodded, allowing Grits to help her to her feet. Grabbing her bags, she steadied herself. He watched her shift from grieving friend to hardened survivor. No, a warrior.

With resolve, she nodded again. "Let's go."

He looked at Salty, a fiery grin on his face. "See you on the flip side."

"See ya, boss. The keys are in the ignition."

Grits moved with purpose, vigilance etched into every step as he approached the truck. No room for surprises now. He and Ava slipped into the battered, rusty pickup, tossing their bags onto the middle of the bench seat with quick, practiced motions. It figured that Salty would have something without GPS.

Salty must've anticipated someone would track them, and he arrived to help them retreat from the location.

He shoved the gear into Reverse, tires throwing dirt as he sped out of the long driveway, casting nervous glances over his shoulder, eyes sharp for any threat lurking in the shadows. Once on the main road, he shifted gears and accelerated, adrenaline pushing him forward.

He grabbed his phone and swiftly dialed the HIS emergency line.

Stone's calm voice responded immediately. "Sitrep."

"Daylan's down. We need Life Flight and a cleanup crew." Grits listened as the keyboard clicked rapidly as Stone took action.

"Alpha team just returned and is on standby."

"Make sure Pup is with them."

"Your status?"

"Oscar Mike with the package." Recalling Salty's words about tracking the phone, he ended the call, rolled down the truck window, and tossed the phone out.

They were definitely on the move to a location that only he, Ava, and Salty would know. He wasn't even going to tell Jesse this time. It suddenly struck him that he hadn't given Stone the address. But then again, Stone knew Jesse had it, and brevity had been the priority in that quick conversation.

CHAPTER FIFTEEN

They sat quietly at a small table tucked in the back corner of the bustling café, their eyes anxiously flicking toward the door, waiting for Grits' friend, Salty. The memory of the large man emerging from the living room shadows still haunted her. Her heart hammered in her chest as panic surged through her. She had fleetingly believed the enemy had finally found them.

"What about Buddy?" Her voice trembled slightly. She'd already asked if he thought Daylan would be okay, several times, each inquiry growing more desperate, annoyingly pressing for reassurance.

He took a sip of his black coffee. "That's why I asked for Pup. He and his wife are the other K9 handlers on the teams, so Buddy's comfortable with them and trusts them."

She nodded, forcing herself to appear composed. "Okay," she managed, though her insides twisted with fear. Deep down, she wondered how they had found them. Again.

She fidgeted nervously with the napkin tucked under her iced tea, her mind racing. "Do you think Salty is okay?" They had been on the road for about an hour after leaving the cabin, yet the anxious hours at the café dragged on, each minute feeling longer than the last. Her stomach knotted at the thought that he might have been caught by their enemy. She couldn't shake the fear that Salty and Daylan hadn't made it out alive.

Noticing her fretful fidgeting, he reached across the table, gently taking her hand in his. His touch was steady, reassuring. "He'll be fine. They both will be. Life Flight would've arrived in time for Daylan. My team has returned, so they would've swooped in to get Salty out of there before the cops even knew what was happening."

"Why call the police at all? Weren't you saying they'd just clean up the mess afterward?" She frowned, unsure. That meant they'd have to make sure Celeb's cabin was back to normal, despite the bullet holes marring the log walls.

He hesitated. "Because Daylan was shot. Bullet wounds need a police report."

"Oh…I see." She nodded slowly, though her concern lingered. They were trying to stay off the radar, after all. Yet, now that the police were involved, everything felt even more complicated.

"Tell me about Salty. What's he like? Will he help keep us safe?" She couldn't help but say "us," as if their lives were somehow intertwined in this chaos that was her world.

Grits glanced at the door before answering, a playful smirk on his face. "First off, know that he's the biggest conspiracy theorist there is." He chuckled. "And he believes Bigfoot is real."

She raised an eyebrow, teasing. "He is, isn't he?"

Startled, Grits blinked. "What?"

She grinned, laughing softly to cut through the tension. "I'm just joking." It felt good to find a moment of lightness amid the crisis.

Grits shook his head, a mixture of exasperation and affection. "What am I supposed to do with you, sweetheart?"

She smiled at that nickname, warmth spreading in her chest. She could get used to it. Now for the billion-dollar question. "Where exactly are we headed?"

Grits shrugged nonchalantly, glancing at the door once more. "It's out in the middle of nowhere. I couldn't find it even if I tried."

Out in the middle of nowhere sounded perfect to her. "Do you think they'll find us this time?" Her heart hammered in her chest at the thought. When would she finally be safe? What if they never decrypted the message? That was a terrifying possibility she couldn't ignore.

"Doubtful. But if they do, they'll have their work cut out for them."

She frowned, sure that confusion flickered across her face. "What do you mean?"

"The land around his cabin is rigged with booby-traps and guarded by enough cameras that even a bird can't land undetected." He took a cautious sip of his coffee, setting the cup down with a measured pause. "That's why we can't go there directly. Only Salty can get us in without trouble."

"What if an innocent walks straight into one of his traps?"

Grits scoffed, a sardonic smile twisting his lips. "Out there, no one would innocently stumble into his lair. It's too dangerous, too calculated."

She still worried about the wildlife and innocent bystanders, but secretly, a sense of relief washed over her. This time, they'd be so well protected. Plus, with two former Navy SEALs watching her back, she couldn't help but feel a flicker of safety ignite inside her. But only a flicker. She couldn't shake the feeling that they would have to run again, and that terrified her.

She ached to dive into the code, but Grits had firmly forbidden her from using the local Wi-Fi, and without their phone, she was stranded without a hotspot. Frustration gnawed at her as she waited, her hopes pinned on reaching Salty's cabin.

Grits kept a watchful eye on the door, a sly smile creeping onto her face. She turned in time to see Salty step out of a car, wave off someone, and stride into the café. He nodded politely to the waitress before making his way back to their table.

He settled into the seat beside Grits, both of them with their backs against the wall, and let out a deep sigh. "Your team is no-nonsense."

Grits beamed with pride, nodding eagerly. "They're the best. Just outside the teams." This time, she knew the teams meant Navy SEALs and not where he worked now.

Salty chuckled, accepting a steaming cup of coffee from Martha, who smiled warmly at him. "Thanks, Martha."

"You're welcome." She turned to walk away. Ava

couldn't help but notice the way Salty watched her, a flicker of longing in his eyes.

She couldn't wait to get past the small talk. She leaned in close. "How's Daylan?" Her voice was low, guarded. She knew in the crowded room that no one else could overhear, but still….

Salty took a slow sip of his coffee, hesitating before answering. "I won't sugarcoat it. He was in pretty bad shape. But the Life Flight crew? They really knew their stuff. They took good care of him."

Her stomach clenched at the secrecy. She hated that they wouldn't know the full story of Daylan's condition. "What about Buddy?"

"A man took him. He struggled to separate him from Daylan. The dog attempted to board the Life Flight helicopter with its handler. It took some time, but he managed to calm Buddy and get him on HIS's helicopter."

"That's good." She settled back into her chair with a calm, measured sip of her tea. Just as she placed the cup down, Salty finished his coffee in one long, deliberate gulp, the burn of it likely catching the back of his throat, and maybe even down his esophagus.

Salty clunked his cup down. "Are you ready?"

Grits chuckled, a low, knowing sound. "Damn, man. We'd have given you time to savor that."

"No." His eyes narrowed toward the doorway. "We need to move. You've already stayed here too long."

Ava's stomach clenched with fear. Were they truly in danger here? No one knew where they had gone unless someone had followed, and Grits had assured her they hadn't been followed.

She wasn't ready to run again, her heart pounding in her chest. "How did you get here?"

Salty shifted slightly, a sly grin creeping on his face. "HIS gave me a lift on the chopper close, then I called a trusted friend for a ride."

Grits raised an eyebrow, skeptical. "I thought I was your only trusted friend?"

Salty scoffed, a spark of mischief in his eyes. "After you never call or visit? I had to find a new friend."

Ava's stomach clenched at the idea of another location betrayal. "Is it someone we can trust?" Her voice wavered, betraying her worry. Maybe they should move—now.

Salty nodded confidently. "Wholeheartedly."

Tension clung thick in the air, like a storm ready to explode, but Ava refused to let it shake her. Her gaze sharpened with determination as she prepared to lead the way to safety. Rising to her feet, she looked at the men. "Let's go, then."

Grits chuckled softly, the kind of sound that eased some of the rising panic. He moved around the table, coming to stand beside her. With a gentle, reassuring gesture, he brushed her hair back and pressed a tender kiss to her temple. "We're going to be fine, sweetheart."

That simple word sent a flutter through her stomach—an uneasy mix of comfort and confusion. She knew it wasn't love. They'd just met, after all, and she didn't believe in love at first sight. Yet, something about him stirred a strange tenderness. Perhaps the chaos he was shielding her from, or a spark of something unexpected.

Whatever it was, she resolved to keep her heart open and see where this strange, dangerous ride might lead.

Grits grabbed his wallet, slapping some bills onto the table with a quick flick of his wrist. "Let go, then."

Salty nodded and led the way out, pausing briefly to exchange a rapid word with Martha. She watched him leave, something glittering in her eyes. Was she trustworthy? It was clear to her that there was more than just friendship between them. Could they even be lovers? As long as she kept their location secret, she didn't care what they were to each other.

Outside, at the truck, they hurriedly tossed their bags into the pickup's bed. With Ava nestled snugly between them on the bench seat, they left the café behind, racing toward whatever lay ahead.

Driving for another twenty minutes or so, they finally veered off the main road onto a narrow, unassuming side path that Ava hadn't even noticed at first. Soon, they arrived at a weathered gate bearing a chilling sign: "No trespassing," and beneath it, in bold, threatening letters, "Trespassers will be shot."

Ava hesitated, uncertain about the second warning, but secretly liked the edge it brought. Maybe it was her way of feeling protected, as long as it wasn't an innocent party.

Salty reached into his pocket and handed Grits a key. Grits hopped out of the truck, approached the gate with a determined stride, and deftly unlocked it. With a quick toss of the chain, he swung the gate open, revealing the mysterious path beyond. After they drove through, Grits took a moment to close and lock the gate again, ensuring their secret was safe before pressing onward into the unknown.

Once off the main road, they continued driving for another ten minutes through the dense woods before Salty suddenly stopped the truck. Salty pulled into a secluded clearing surrounded by towering trees and thick brush.

Ava strained her eyes, searching for any sign of his cabin, but all she saw was nature's unspoiled wilderness. "Where's your cabin?"

Salty turned to her with a small, secretive smile before stepping out of the vehicle. "It's a bit of a hike."

Ava's stomach clenched at the thought of hiking deeper into the woods. She wasn't comfortable with the idea, especially knowing the critters that scurried and crawled among the trees. An unsettling shudder ran down her spine as she imagined tiny legs crawling on her skin, sending a chill through her.

The men exited the truck, and she quickly scrambled after them, heart pounding. Grits pulled out a flashlight, then threw his backpack over his shoulder and grabbed her bags in one swift motion. Ava peered into the darkness, noticing Salty don a backpack tucked away in the back of the truck that she hadn't seen before. How were they supposed to see anything in these pitch-black woods?

Salty activated a flashlight with a red light instead of the usual bright beam. Was that really going to help them navigate through the dense woods and dodge hidden booby-traps? She had her doubts.

Reaching out her hand, she looked at Grits. "I need a real flashlight."

He hesitated, studying her. After a moment, he

nodded, but just before handing it over, he fiddled with the bulb, changing something. Smiling mysteriously, he handed her the device. "There you go."

Relieved, she clicked it on, only to discover it emitted the same eerie red glow. Who did these men think would be hiding in the woods, caught in the shadows? The darkness seemed to close in around her, thicker and more threatening than ever.

Salty pushed through the thick brush. "Let's do this."

In the moonlight, she caught Grits' furrowed brow as he looked at her with concern. "Are you okay, Ava?"

Was she? No, not really. Someone wanted her dead, and now she was following someone who believed Bigfoot was real. What could possibly go wrong? She forced a smile. "Yes," she lied, not wanting Grits to see her trembling inside.

"Then, let's go." Grits urged her forward into the eerie woods. The shadows around them seemed alive, concealing danger behind every tree. This wasn't just a walk. It was a race against the unknown. Fear gripped her, tighter than ever, as she wondered if they would make it out. Maybe this hellish trek was only the beginning of something far worse. But honestly, was there anything more terrifying than someone trying to kill her?

CHAPTER SIXTEEN

Grits could tell Ava wasn't exactly enjoying their trek through the woods. Honestly, neither was he. The darkness was thick, and the memories of those earlier attempts on their lives still haunted him. No wonder they were both a little on edge.

He watched her brush away invisible or perhaps real bugs, a small, amused smile tugging at the corners of his lips. It was a funny sight, though he couldn't help but feel a twinge of sympathy. Despite his special ops training, creepy crawlies still didn't sit well with him either. He secretly hoped Salty had his exterminator duties well in hand.

They had been walking for about twenty minutes. The anticipation of reaching their destination was building. Any moment now, they'd arrive.

Salty came to a sudden stop, raising a fist in warning just as Ava charged forward into Salty's back.

Alarmed, Grits hurried to catch up, quickly covering her mouth to silence any questions.

Lowering his voice to a tense whisper, Salty warned, "We're almost there. Just watch your step from here."

But how were they supposed to watch their footing in

the near pitch dark? He'd already handed over his flashlight to Ava, leaving himself walking blind. Fortunately, the woods weren't so thick that moonlight couldn't filter through in faint glimmers, revealing glimpses of those in front of him.

Ava nodded, and Grits gently lowered his hand from her mouth. A mouth he'd been kissing not so long ago. The memory flickered in his mind, feeling like a lifetime ago, especially after the harrowing escape from the drones and their mysterious enemies.

His heart still pounding, he leaned closer and whispered, "It's okay. Just follow in his footsteps." Though she had a tactical flashlight that would make that simple for her, he wasn't as lucky. He silently hoped he wouldn't accidentally step on something that could ruin the rest of his day.

Within minutes, a shadowy structure emerged in the dim light. It was a cabin. Not the cozy log one Celeb owned, but still standing firm and reliable, faintly taking shape in the darkness. Relief washed over him, but he knew their journey was far from over.

Several times, Salty paused to disable a booby trap here, then another there. Each time, he'd loop back behind Grits, reattach the device, and then march forward with renewed purpose. As they neared the cabin, Salty halted their progress once more. Silently, he slipped inside, gun at the ready, to investigate. Grits watched, puzzled, wondering what had driven his friend to this point.

Salty, always the conspiracy theorist of the teams, tended to see shadowy plots lurking behind every corner.

Now, with this isolated cabin and its deadly traps, Grits couldn't help but think of how far Salty had gone this time. Had he truly lost touch with reality? It looked like his friend had crossed a line and gone over the edge into full-blown paranoia.

So, the question lingered—could they really trust him? Grits doubted Salty would betray them. After all, he wouldn't want anyone to discover his secret hideaway. But whether Salty's help was reliable was where Grits found himself stuck.

They had at least a safe place to lie low while Ava worked on cracking the code. That was assuming Salty's setup was up to the task. Did he even have internet out here? Maybe there was a satellite dish hidden somewhere, bringing the world to their little refuge.

A generator coughed to life, then Salty flicked on the lights, swung open the door, and gestured invitingly inside. Ava stepped forward first, then froze mid-step, blocking Grits' path. He glanced over her shoulder and froze. The room was a high-tech command center, boasting a sleek computer setup with multiple monitors. Some displayed live security camera feeds, others flickered with lines of code and digital maps.

His curiosity piqued, Grits looked around further. One entire wall was plastered with newspaper clippings of conspiracy theories and wild headlines haphazardly covering every inch.

Ava, seemingly snapping out of her trance, pressed on inside, stopping just as Grits entered beside her.

Grits gently wrapped his arm around Ava's shoulders. "Thanks again, Salty. You have no idea what this means to me. To us." He cast a loving glance down at Ava, who smiled up at him, probably appreciating the inclusion of "us" and not just himself. Women.

Salty shrugged casually. "Don't think twice about it. You needed help, and I'm here for that. Lord knows, you've saved my ass enough times out there."

Grits chuckled. "Honestly, I think it was the other way around."

Salty nodded toward the back. "Anyway, I've got an extra room. You two can crash there. Just need to freshen up the sheets." With a grin, he disappeared into the tiny kitchen, pulling water from the fridge. He handed each of them a bottle. "Hydrate."

Grits grinned, realizing it wasn't just a suggestion. He opened his bottle, then traded with Ava, both taking long, thirst-quenching drinks. The hike had left him parched, and he drank deeply, feeling the cool relief wash over him.

"Salty," Ava began, "how on earth did you set all this up out here? And how secure is it?"

Salty grinned with pride. "It's the most secure place you'll find outside the CIA. And out here, I've got a dish hidden deep in the woods."

Grits raised an eyebrow, thinking that might reveal someone was living out here. But then again, who would go this far off the beaten path? Only hunters and maybe the occasional adventurer, but the gate should keep anyone out.

Grits led Ava to the back of the cabin, arriving at the room he suspected Salty had set aside for them. The space featured a double bed and sparse furniture. It was a far cry from what he'd prefer for Ava, but it would suffice. Still, he couldn't help but wonder how he'd fit his six-foot-one frame onto the bed without his feet dangling over the edge. At least he'd be close to Ava, which was all that mattered.

Suddenly, Salty appeared behind them, carrying a pair of sheets that caught Grits off guard.

"Are these bamboo sheets?"

His friend nodded with a faint smile. "Even if I'm out of the public eye, I still like my creature comforts."

Grits had expected rugged, military-issued sheets—hard as cardboard—but these luxurious bamboo sheets were a pleasant surprise, and he accepted the gesture with gratitude.

Ava began stripping the bed, her eyes scanning for any lurking spiders. He knew the truth that out here, spiders were just part of the landscape.

Salty watched her, a grin spreading across his face. "Don't worry, ma'am." He chuckled. "I spray myself to keep the critters outside where they belong." He shrugged. "Not like I'd trust any service out here anyhow."

Salty handed him a comforter still sealed in its plastic wrap. The rugged man shrugged. "I figured someone might need this place at some point."

Grits watched his friend, feeling a wave of sympathy. Living off the grid, even with satellite internet, couldn't be easy. He wondered how Salty kept his system secure. Ava would soon find out. He was sure of it.

"Get some shut-eye, you two. Tomorrow's a new day."

Grits checked his watch. It was already past three a.m. No way they'd get much sleep tonight, especially after the adrenaline of the evening. Still, they needed to try. He placed his empty weapon on the nightstand. He'd have to get ammo from Salty in the morning.

Silent, they finished making the bed, turned off the light, slipped off their shoes, and sank into the quiet comfort of the room. Ava immediately curled up on his shoulder, her breathing calming as he gently wrapped his arm around her. In that moment, everything felt right. Not hiding in the woods or fleeing mercenaries, this simple closeness was what mattered. He leaned in and kissed her temple. "How are you holding up?"

She remained silent for a moment. With the moonlight filtering through the window, he watched her closely, feeling a surge of curiosity and concern. Suddenly, a flicker of fire ignited in her eyes—a spark that nearly unraveled him. "I'm angry," she finally whispered, "and I'm scared."

He nodded gently, understanding the weight behind her words. "You have every right to be both." Her admission of fear was a significant step. He knew trust was slow to build for her, and opening up wasn't easy.

"Do you think we can trust this—place?"

He noticed her hesitation—she didn't say "person," only "place." The sight of the computer system clearly unsettled her more than she let on. That realization sent a sharp jolt through him, intensifying his protectiveness and resolve.

"Yes, I believe we're as safe as we can be for now. You can check his system in the morning and see how secure it is before diving back into the code." He leaned in and planted a gentle kiss on her lips. "By the way, Salty had been studying cryptology while on the teams. Did I mention that?"

Her eyes widened. "Really? Do you think he could help us?"

Grits smiled softly, kissing her again with a tenderness that lingered. "Maybe. We'll see how it goes in the morning." He pulled her closer. "So, are you ready to get some sleep?"

Ava shook her head, a reluctant smile playing on her lips. "Probably not yet."

He leaned in, eyes glinting with mischief. "Then I've got just the thing to make sure we're both tired enough."

She straightened, tense. "With your friend in the other room?"

He chuckled softly, confidence in his voice. "He probably already suspects what's happening between us. Just remember, as long as you don't scream my name at the top of your lungs, we'll be just fine."

A naughty grin curled on her lips. "Oh, I'll scream your name. Will I?"

His smile widened. "That's a promise."

She leaned into him. "That's a promise I expect you to fulfill."

He drew her into his embrace, holding her close as their eyes locked in a lingering gaze. With a tender motion, he brushed her hair away from her face, revealing a smile that lit up the moment. Leaning in, his lips found hers in a gentle, exploratory kiss, each movement filled with curiosity and longing. The kiss was a perfect blend of passion and tenderness, expressing a deep desire to connect, as he savored the softness of her lips with both gentleness and a hint of urgency.

A low, guttural groan escaped from his throat, echoing the mix of desire and frustration within him. His lips suddenly pressed fiercely against hers, capturing her in a passionate kiss that was both urgent and commanding. As his mouth parted hers, his tongue smoothly slipped inside, exploring her with a bold, heated insistence. The sensation ignited a fiery sensation within his body, a burning sensation that spread through every fiber of his being, intensifying the moment's intensity.

Breaking free to catch his breath, he gently pressed his forehead against hers.

"Ava," he whispered, his voice hoarse with desire, "if you want to stop, you'd better say so now, because I really don't want to stop."

She hesitated for a moment, then smiled. "What about the line?" she teased.

He chuckled softly, eyes shimmering. "Fuck the line."

Her giggle was all the encouragement he needed. "Well, okay then. Kiss on."

He closed the gap between them, their breaths mingling as the world outside faded away.

CHAPTER SEVENTEEN

Ava surrendered herself completely to the intense passion of the kiss, her heart pounding with eager anticipation. This moment was something she had desired more than anything else in the world. She couldn't quite pinpoint when he had shifted from being just her bodyguard to someone more—someone she longed for intimately.

As his lips moved softly yet insistently over hers, her pulse fluttered wildly, and a fiery heat erupted within her, spreading through her with exhilarating intensity. It had been quite some time since she last shared an intimate moment with someone, but she couldn't deny that the intense heat and desire she felt at that very moment were unlike anything she'd experienced before, rushing over her with unexpected speed and fervor.

As his hand slowly slid up her side and under her shirt, his fingers tracing a gentle path, he tenderly cupped her breast, eliciting a soft moan of pleasure from her lips. His touch was electric, like a firebrand searing across her skin, setting every nerve alight with sensation.

He gently broke the kiss, whispering a soft, "Shh," against her lips, urging her to quiet her eager responses. In response, she passionately captured his mouth with her own, her lips pressing firmly over his, conveying the depth of her desire and longing for him.

When his thumb brushed against her nipple, a wave of desire surged through her, and she felt the urge to moan once more. However, she restrained herself, knowing that she didn't want to face their friend in the morning with flushed cheeks from embarrassment.

Feeling an overwhelming urge to connect with him physically, she gently slid her hand down his rock-hard chest, her fingers yearning to trace the intricate tattoos that adorned his skin. However, she resisted the temptation and continued her descent, her hand finally reaching and grasping his length. This time, it was he who let out a deep, resonant moan.

She paused their kiss, playfully mimicking his soft "Shh," and then let out a light giggle.

"Woman, you drive me crazy."

She smiled, her eyes twinkling with mischief. "It could be worse."

Reclaiming her lips with fervor, he pulled her closer, pressing her against him so tightly that their trapped hands could no longer move. As if suddenly aware of this constraint, he eased up slightly, allowing his hand to travel from her chest down her stomach, exploring every curve with a tender yet urgent touch.

His lips left hers, leaving a trail of intense heat that sizzled down her chest, each touch igniting a spark of desire. With a gentle yet firm motion, he lifted her shirt, carefully shifting her bra aside, his lips brushing against her nipple with a tantalizing sense of possessiveness that sent shivers down her spine. A low growl rumbled from his chest, a sound filled with frustration and longing, as he muttered, "Too damn many clothes."

She nodded in agreement, her own desire urging her to act. With a swift motion, she released him and pulled her shirt over her head, eager to shed the layers that separated them. Sensing her urgency, he stood up from the bed, his movements fluid and deliberate. He ripped his shirt off with a restless urgency, baring his chest in one motion. His pants and boxers followed, each garment discarded with a sense of liberation.

Under the warmth of the covers, she slithered out of her jeans and underwear, her skin now bare against the soft fabric. With practiced ease, she unclasped her bra and tossed it aside, feeling a sense of freedom and anticipation.

He returned to the bed, his eyes locked on her as he pulled the covers back, revealing her fully to his gaze. He drank in the sight of her with a hunger that was palpable, his eyes tracing the curves of her body with a mix of admiration and desire.

As the thick, heavy clouds obscured the moonlight, the room was enveloped in a deep, impenetrable darkness. Yet, she was intimately familiar with his presence, needing no light to visualize him. Her hands rested gently against his chest, feeling the steady rhythm of his heartbeat. He drew her closer, this time allowing for a more deliberate and exploratory connection.

No longer was he moving with a languid, leisurely pace. He had intensified the moment, his hand now moving with purpose and urgency to her core. In response, she reached down, her fingers wrapping around his length, feeling the tension build within him.

A low, primal growl rumbled in his throat, a sound that threatened to break free. To silence it, she pressed her lips against his, sealing them in a passionate kiss that served as a reminder of the promise he had made to her.

With his fingers, he skillfully teased and tormented her core and clit, sending a firestorm of sensations coursing through her body. Her desire for him was intense, and she felt an overwhelming need to be with him at that very moment.

"Condom?"

"Damn." He quickly jumped off the bed. He reached for his pants, rummaging through his pockets before pulling out his wallet. With practiced hands, he removed a condom, carefully rolling it on before settling back on top of her. "I want to make love with you all night, Ava, but I can't guarantee this first time will be my best."

She grinned, her eyes sparkling with mischief and affection. "But you made a promise."

Leaning in closer, he whispered against her lips, his voice soft yet filled with determination. "Oh, I intend to keep that promise."

Reaching down with a gentle yet firm touch, she guided him to her entrance, feeling the anticipation build between them. As he entered her, she arched her back, welcoming him with a slow and reassuring motion. Each small thrust brought them closer, and she felt a wave of overwhelming pleasure wash over her, almost to the point of madness.

"You are so damn tight."

Overwhelmed by the moment's intensity, she found herself speechless, unable to respond. Instead, she expressed her emotions through a series of tender kisses along his throat, savoring the warmth and closeness of their bodies. Their lips met again in a fiery kiss, a passionate and consuming embrace that made all previous kisses seem like mere teenage foreplay.

As they surrendered completely to the passionate rhythm of lovemaking, her climax began to intensify. Initially, it was a gentle, simmering sensation, but soon the fire within her body started to blaze, eager to be unleashed. She wrapped her legs tightly around his thighs, drawing him even closer, while he silenced her moan with a deep, consuming kiss.

Pausing for a moment to catch her breath, she whispered, "I'm close."

He responded with a relieved and fervent, "Thank God, because I am too."

With their foreheads gently touching, they were enveloped in the soft, silvery glow of the moonlight, which cast a serene, intimate atmosphere around them. She gazed up into his eyes, feeling the intense, raw heat of his gaze as he smiled down at her, a smile that spoke volumes of his affection and desire.

As she continued to rise, her body moved to a rhythm both powerful and graceful, climbing higher and higher until the fire within her reached its peak. In that moment, she felt herself break into fiery shards, a dazzling display of passion and release as she reached the pinnacle of her ecstasy.

He groaned deeply, thrusting into her with renewed

vigor before he finally stilled, his body throbbing within her, a testament to the intensity of their shared experience.

He collapsed beside her, his breathing ragged and uneven. "I have to dispose of this condom." His voice was barely audible over the gentle rustle of the sheets.

She paused, realizing the predicament they were in. There was no en-suite bathroom in this room, which meant he would have to either find a discreet place to discard the condom in the bedroom or risk walking out with it in front of Salty.

"Don't worry. There's a garbage can in here, and I'll make sure Salty doesn't see it in the morning."

His words were meant to comfort her, though she couldn't shake the feeling that Salty was already aware of their intimate activities. However, she preferred not to have it confirmed outright.

He rose from the bed momentarily, moving quietly to locate the trash can. Once he found it, he returned to her side, pulling her gently into his arms. He pressed a tender kiss to the top of her head, his touch both soothing and affectionate.

"Sleep, my sweet."

She slipped into a tranquil sleep, the worries of assassins and spiders vanishing from her mind. In her dreams, she envisioned their passionate lovemaking and glimpsed the possibilities that the future might hold for them, filled with hope and promise.

Ava woke to golden light bleeding through the cabin windows and the distant sound of birdsong. For a second —just one—it felt like they were anywhere but hunted.

Grits was already up, standing by the bed with his jaw

tight. He was shirtless, muscles tense, the gun holstered at his hip again like the night they'd just shared hadn't happened at all.

She sat up, the sheet pulling across her chest. "You're back to full tactical mode."

He didn't turn around. "It's not a choice, Ava."

She studied his back, the way his shoulders moved with tightly coiled restraint. "You didn't wake me."

"You looked peaceful."

"I'm not." Her voice was soft but steady. "Because now I'm wondering if last night changed anything or if you're already regretting it."

He turned, and his expression flickered—something unreadable in his eyes before he looked away.

"Say something."

He crossed to the window, silent for a beat. Then, "This was never supposed to happen."

Ava's stomach sank. "Wow."

"You were a job. A target to protect. I crossed a line I never should have. And now you're not just in danger from the people hunting you—you're in danger because I couldn't keep my distance."

She slipped out of bed, wrapping the sheet around her. "So what, Grits? That's it? We go back to pretending this didn't mean anything?"

His voice rose. "It means everything. That's the problem."

She froze.

"I feel like I'm already too deep in." His voice was raw now, cracking. "You make me forget the mission. Make me want things I swore I'd never risk again. You're not just under my skin, Ava. You're in me. And that scares the hell out of me. You're like the air, surrounding me and floating through my soul."

Her chest tightened. "Then why push me away?"

"Because I don't want to be the reason you get killed."

Her eyes shimmered, but she held her ground. "You're not."

He looked at her then, like he was seeing her for the first time—not as a job, or a responsibility, but as a woman who had survived just as much as he had.

"I don't want to regret this. But if you walk out of this room and decide what we had was a mistake, I will."

He didn't answer right away. But then he crossed the room, stopped in front of her, and pressed his forehead to hers. "This is the part where I don't know how to be brave."

She closed her eyes. "Then be scared. Just don't lie to me."

"That, Ava, I can promise you won't happen."

CHAPTER EIGHTEEN

Grits couldn't believe he'd spilled his deepest fear to Ava about their fragile relationship. What had driven him to voice such vulnerability? The answer was simple— Ava. She was so deeply embedded in his soul that the thought of losing her was unbearable. Yet beneath that fear lay another: the uncertainty of their situation and of how to keep her safe without HIS support. Salty might have been a seasoned warrior, hardened by countless battles, but he knew he wasn't a one-man army. He needed backup, and he needed it now.

The thought of Daylan sent a shiver down his spine, a gripping fear for the man's health. Their last encounter hadn't been promising, and he desperately hoped Daylan had pulled through. The agent's fierce defense of Ava was proof enough that he wasn't the leak, but someone else was, and he needed to uncover the traitor before reaching out to HQ again. For now, they would remain invisible to everyone.

Salty handed him a steaming cup of black coffee. "Still taking it like this, LT?"

Grits quickly interjected, not wanting Salty to revert to his old SEAL persona with Grits as his commanding officer. He wanted them to be equals. "I'm just Grits now. No LT."

Salty nodded, a hint of a smile playing on his lips. "Habit." He took a long sip from his coffee mug. "So, what's the game plan?"

Grits, feeling the heat of the coffee spread through him, remembered just how strong Salty liked his brew. "Well, she's going to check your system first."

Salty's posture tensed. "No one touches my system."

"Chill out. She's a top-notch cybersecurity expert. She just needs to make sure everything's secure before she starts cracking the code."

Salty's eyebrows shot up. "Did you just say 'cracking the code'?"

Grits chuckled, enjoying the reaction. "I knew that would get your attention."

As he recounted the events to Salty, Ava stepped out of the room, her hair tied back in a sleek ponytail and wearing a fresh outfit. Her makeup-free face was striking, and he found himself captivated by her natural beauty.

Salty beamed at her. "Would you like some coffee, ma'am?"

Ava glanced at Grits, who shook his head. She would not be a fan of Salty's potent brew.

"No thanks. I'm eager to dive in."

Salty glanced at Grits, who gave a reassuring nod.

With that, Salty began to unveil the intricacies of his system to Ava. The jargon flew over Grits' head, so he decided to wander through the living area and delve into Salty's intriguing wall of theories. There it was— Q'Anon, Deep State, the JFK assassination, Princess

Diana's tragic end, and a host of other mysteries. Salty was a true believer, seemingly on a mission to crack some of these enigmas. But the alien tales from Area 51? Grits dismissed them entirely.

As he roamed the room, Grits' eyes fell upon photos capturing moments of triumph and camaraderie with the team after intense missions in South America and the Middle East. These memories were precious, yet they tugged at Grits' heartstrings. As their former commander, he bore the weight of losing three men under his leadership. It wasn't his choices that led to their deaths, just the cruel twist of fate orchestrated by the terrorists.

In a shocking turn of events, the team was caught off guard by a sudden ambush while en route to their target, leading to the heartbreaking loss of three of the men involved. This devastating blow prompted an immediate recall of the original team to evaluate the situation and chart a new path forward. Undeterred, a fresh team was swiftly assembled and dispatched to carry on the mission, determined to achieve their objectives despite the unexpected challenge.

The new team had been riding high on success, while Grits found himself in the somber role of comforting grieving families. After the cover-up, he'd lost his appetite for government work and eventually parted ways with the Navy. With his unique skills, he was recruited by Matt Hamilton, a fellow SEAL, into HIS. It was a perfect match. Though it was challenging to step back from leading and instead follow, he learned to adapt and thrive. Then, he finally got his own team.

Would he let them down, too? This thought always

shadowed him during operations. So far, they had triumphed, and everyone had returned home safely.

The weight of responsibility pressed heavily on him as he grappled with the decision that had led to a Charlie team member risking his life to protect Grit's charge. Whether Daylan survived or not, the outcome rested solely on his shoulders. Could he endure the burden of another loss? He turned away from the haunting photos, knowing he might have to. Yet, deep down, he clung to the hope that it wouldn't come to that.

Ava and Salty were absorbed in their work on the computer system, leaving him feeling adrift. Typically, he would reach out to HQ for updates, gather new intelligence, and strategize his next steps. But now, he was without the guidance he needed to make that crucial move.

Anticipating a quiet morning, he made his way to the kitchen, hoping Salty had some breakfast ingredients. With a plan in mind, he started preparing a hearty meal of eggs, bacon, and grits for everyone.

"Since when did you become a grits fan, Salty?"

Salty glanced up from his computer, a hint of amusement in his eyes. "Oh, I'm not. They're just shelf-stable, so I keep them around since oatmeal isn't my thing."

They had plenty of oatmeal in their breakfast MREs, enough to make him dread having oatmeal again.

While the kitchen was filled with an abundance of food, he felt guilty intruding. "Salty, I don't want to eat all your food."

Salty waved him off with a reassuring smile. "Don't

worry, I picked up some groceries after you called."

Relief washed over him, knowing they were well-stocked for the days ahead. He'd reimburse his friend before they parted ways.

Tearing Ava and Salty away from the computer was a challenge, but he knew it was crucial for Ava to fuel up before diving into the day's mission of cracking the code. As they gathered around the breakfast table, their excitement was palpable, buzzing with theories about the code's origins and the countries it might represent. China seemed to be the frontrunner, but Grits couldn't shake the feeling that it was just a wild guess. Then again, he mused, his instincts had often led him to success in the past.

As he watched Ava's excitement, Grits felt a whirlwind of emotions. He was utterly captivated by her, head over heels. Could this blossom into something more? He had no idea, but he was eager to find out—after he helped her through this. A knot twisted in his gut. What if he couldn't protect her? What if they failed to crack the code and unmask the culprit before it was too late? They couldn't keep living their lives in constant fear of assassins lurking around every corner.

Salty squinted at Grits. "What's going on in that mind of yours?"

Grits shook off the somber thoughts, determined to be truthful, as he had promised Ava never to lie. "I'm just wondering how long we have here?"

"As long as you need, LT."

Grits didn't correct him this time. Old habits die hard. "Thanks, Salty. But won't someone notice you buying more groceries than normal?" It was the little things that could trip people up when they were on the run.

Salty grinned, his eyes twinkling with mischief. "Went to a different grocery store." He shook his head, a playful glint in his eye. "Come on, LT. This isn't my first rodeo."

Grits needed information, and before Salty and Ava vanished into their digital realm, he had to ask the right questions. "Tell me about the perimeter."

With a confident posture and a voice full of purpose, Salty launched into his explanation, "There are cameras scattered throughout the woods, visible on those screens." He gestured toward the monitors lining the wall.

Grits quickly counted around over twenty small squares, realizing there were plenty of cameras. That was a lot of territory covered. "What about the traps?"

Salty grinned widely, his pride shining through. "They're strategically positioned near the cabin, ensuring no one can approach without being aware they shouldn't."

"What about emergency egress? Won't they be a problem?"

Salty shook his head. "I've got a small, secret path that's clear. But you need to know it. If we have to make a quick getaway, you'll need me to lead the way."

Grits hadn't initially planned to bring Salty along if they had to flee at a moment's notice, but the thought of stumbling into a booby trap made him reconsider. "What about transportation? Is it just the truck?"

Salty chuckled, a hint of mischief in his eyes. "Ah, come on, LT. What do you take me for? Two more trucks are strategically parked along the egress route. Both are fully stocked for a fast escape."

"But what about for the three of us?"

Salty nodded, his assurance unwavering. "I've already packed enough for three in each vehicle."

Salty had thought this through more thoroughly than Grits could have imagined. He had come to save their skins, and Grits knew he owed this man more than he could ever repay.

He needed absolute certainty. To visually confirm their route, the transportation, and the contents of the go-bags. "Show me."

Salty cast a longing glance at the computer before turning back to Grits. "Sure thing."

Grits grinned reassuringly. "Don't worry. You'll have plenty of time to play on the computer."

With a nod, Salty got up. "Let me get the dishes."

Grits stood, stopping him. "I'll get them. You make sure she's ready to go, then we'll take that walk."

Salty nodded. "I can do that."

As his friend and Ava resumed their conversation about codes, he found himself lost. He sighed, carrying the dishes to the sink. No dishwasher here, so hand washing it was. That's what he did at his home since it was just him, even though he had a dishwasher.

Suddenly, it struck him like a bolt of lightning. To take the walk, they'd have to leave Ava behind, and that was simply out of the question. No way, no how. He turned back to them with determination. "Ava, you're coming with us."

Her face lit up with relief, and he understood she had been scared to be alone but didn't want to admit it in front of Salty. He'd need to have a chat with her about speaking up, even when his old teammate was around.

Once the dishes were done, they embarked on their hike through the woods, carefully following the path that would serve as their escape route if they were discovered.

Ava ducked under a low branch. "Aren't you worried someone might come this way?"

Salty shook his head. "They'd have to skirt around the property, which I'd spot on camera, and they'd have to be incredibly cautious. Notice we're not taking a straight line."

Grits couldn't have been prouder of his old teammate than he was as they approached the first vehicle and the go-bags. Salty had truly prepared, and his heart swelled with warmth.

Now, he just had to figure out where their next stop would be if this place was discovered. He was out of secret friends. The only safe place he knew was HIS, but with a leak, they'd find her instantly. So what would he do?

CHAPTER NINETEEN

Ava couldn't believe that these men were already plotting their next move. Exhausted from running and longing to reclaim her life, she realized she had to crack the code or find out who had placed it there for that to happen. Unfortunately, she was doubting herself.

Yet, fortunately, she had Salty, a cryptology expert whose skills rivaled her own. Together, they made an unstoppable team, ready to unravel whatever secrets lay ahead.

She and Salty sat anxiously in front of the computer, eyes glued to the flickering screen, both deeply puzzled about their next move. Suddenly, Salty snapped his fingers. "I've got some keys that might crack a Chinese code or two." Without delay, he slipped into his bedroom, reappearing moments later clutching a worn folder.

Out of nowhere, Grits materialized, a fierce scowl etched on his face. "Where did you get those?"

Salty hesitated, the folder still in his hand. "Relax, LT. I didn't steal anything. These are from my training days. I remembered them."

Although she knew Salty was studying cryptology, she had no idea it was his specialty in the Navy before he became a SEAL. Grits hadn't mentioned that vital piece of information.

"Okay, then."

"But, LT, does it really matter if it's classified or not? That message will have a signature that we might not be able to crack completely, making it hard to figure everything out."

Ava considered his point carefully. Still, she knew that even if they managed to decode the message, they might never uncover who had placed it in the system. The challenge of tracking it was proving far more complicated than she'd anticipated.

Grits paused for a moment, as if a secret message passed silently between the two men. "I understand your point. Just be careful."

She couldn't quite grasp what had just unfolded, but she sensed he was giving them the go-ahead to pursue their goal by any means necessary.

Her identity as a "Red Hat" hacker, where she fearlessly probed company systems to expose vulnerabilities and unmask the pathways "Black Hat" hackers might exploit, defined her skills in that realm. Her relentless curiosity and exceptional skill made her a formidable force in cybersecurity.

Yet, breaking into the government vaults to hunt down a secret key was a whole different game. One she knew was beyond her reach.

Salty, however, grinned like a kid on Christmas, eyes sparkling with excitement.

Grits walked over to her and put a hand on her shoulder. "Are you okay?"

The gentle touch of his fingertips sent a cascade of delicious shivers down her spine, igniting a fiery sensation that spread through her body. Their early morning activities remained vividly fresh in her mind with every tender caress and every whispered word. He had been an exceptional lover, fulfilling every promise with passion and care, making her feel cherished and desired. As she soared to the peak of pleasure, she desperately wanted to scream his name, allowing herself to fully surrender to the overwhelming waves of orgasm.

Their conversation this morning haunted her, echoing in her mind like a ghost she couldn't shake. He truly feared his objectivity had been compromised, worried he might inadvertently get her killed because of it. But she knew better. She wasn't naïve. Plus, Salty was watching their backs, adding a layer of safety she couldn't ignore. She felt relief knowing they had that protection, especially with the leak at HIS looming on the horizon.

Would he truly grasp the courage it takes to seize this chance for them? She hesitated, uncertain. Now wasn't the moment, and they owed a debt to luck and Salty's vigilant watch this morning. Yet, deep down, she couldn't bear the thought of him walking away once the chaos settled.

He gently squeezed her shoulder, his touch reassuring. "Ava?"

Startled from her thoughts, she looked up, her smile soft. "I'm fine." Though inside, she wasn't. Not until she found a way to banish Grits' fear. That might be a battle she couldn't win, and the thought weighed heavily on her heart.

Grits gently pulled his hand away, leaving her feeling unexpectedly adrift. "You two have been at this for hours. How about a quick break for some lunch? There are sandwich fixin's in the fridge and chips on the counter."

She hesitated, reluctant to pause, and Salty looked equally unwilling. Suddenly, her stomach grumbled loudly, betraying her. It was early afternoon, and breakfast had been a distant memory this morning.

Embarrassingly, the men heard her stomach growl and chuckled. A flush of heat swept over her face, betraying her. "Okay, so I could use a bit of food."

She hadn't been able to eat much earlier that morning, her appetite suppressed by the weight of her thoughts. The lingering conversation kept floating to the forefront of her mind, haunting her with every passing moment. He was afraid that much she kept rehashing, replaying the vulnerability he had confided in her. His admission of such a significant risk, of opening up emotionally, made her realize that he must genuinely feel something for her. It wasn't just a casual encounter or chance. She was more than just a job he got lucky with. There was something real behind his actions.

What if she had never uncovered the truth? The thought sent a shiver down her spine.

More than anything, she yearned to reclaim her life, to break free from the endless cycle of fleeing and hiding out. They couldn't stay at Salty's place forever.

She refused to let their lives be dictated by fear any longer.

Ava dreamed of a world where they could stroll hand in hand down the street, free from the shadow of danger.

She longed for moments of intimacy where they could lose themselves in each other, without the need to constantly watch their backs.

She jumped when someone touched her shoulder.

Grits furrowed his brows. "Ava? You with us?"

She brushed aside the melancholy thoughts clouding her mind, offering a fleeting smile. "Yes. And I'm starving." She rose from her seat and followed Salty into the kitchen, Grits trailing close behind. Even inside the house, they formed a protective barrier around her, her perception tinged with the possibility that maybe that was how it was meant to feel.

In the kitchen, she watched as they made sandwiches and piled their plates with chips. They settled at a small table tucked into the nook. Since there were only two chairs, they did the same as for breakfast, dragging the computer chair over. She wondered whether Salty anticipated much company, which prompted her to think about Martha at the café.

Salty seemed to be living a solitary existence, hidden away among his booby traps. Or perhaps he truly enjoyed the peace of solitude. Though she wasn't sure, she genuinely hoped he found happiness in his isolated world.

She listened attentively as Grits and Salty exchanged stories, reminiscing about their intense, adventurous time in the SEALs. Grits chuckled at some of the daring antics and close calls they experienced, their voices filled with camaraderie and nostalgia. However, as the conversation continued, she noticed a flicker of sadness cross Grits' face when he spoke of certain events, revealing that some memories still haunted him. She guessed they might have lost close friends or team members along the way, either due to the inherent dangers of their line of work or simply bad luck. She silently resolved to discuss it more with him later, hoping to offer support or understanding in any way she could, knowing how heavy such memories could be.

She couldn't even begin to fathom the kind of danger they had faced. Danger so intense and perilous that it far outstripped anything she'd known in her own life. Was that why he hesitated, why he kept his distance while acting as her protector? Could he be haunted by the fear of losing someone he cared about again? She refused to let that happen, standing her ground for two powerful reasons: her own life was at stake, and she was determined to uncover who was behind this chaos before anyone else got hurt. That was her relentless hope.

Her curiosity about the nickname burned brightly, almost impossible to ignore. "Why do they call you Salty?"

Salty's cheeks flushed. Or so she thought, given the dim, flickering light of the cabin.

Grits chuckled before answering. "Because he was a salty dawg. And not of the canine variety." His laughter was infectious, and soon Salty was laughing along too.

"It's okay, Ava. I was like that back then."

"And not now?" Her thoughts drifted back to Martha and the longing looks they'd exchanged.

Salty's expression softened as he took a breath. "Not now. No."

"What about Martha?" She regretted the words as they slipped out before she could think.

He straightened, a sigh escaping his lips. "Ain't no one

gonna want to live like this, and I'm not going back into society the way I used to."

As if sensing the shift in the conversation, Grits quickly intervened. "About time you two got back to work. I'll check the perimeter."

"Do you remember where the traps are, LT?"

Grits nodded confidently. "I'm good."

Ava's heart pounded, prickling with fear. What if Grits accidentally triggered a trap? Could she bear to see him get hurt? She darted a glance at the monitors. The screens covered every inch of the woods, relayed by Salty's high-tech setup.

Grits shook his head, a hint of resolve in his eyes. "I need the air."

Ava paused, questioning whether his need was driven by memories of fallen teammates or her and the tense situation at hand. Whatever the reason, she knew she couldn't hold him back.

"Salty, you take care of her while I'm gone."

Salty stood and saluted. "I'll take care of her as if she were my own."

Grits chuckled as he stood. "Carry on, sailor."

"Before you go, LT, let me top off the generator."

Ava wondered what kind of beastly generator Salty had to fuel this high-tech haven. But she kept her questions to herself. Stepping outside for answers wasn't appealing, especially with assassins after her.

"Sure thing." Grits grabbed her plate, carried it to the kitchen, and dumped the napkins into the trash. He then washed the dishes and turned to face her, clearing his throat with a deliberate pause.

She sensed this was her cue. What he was about to say wouldn't be good news.

"About this morning—" he started, and her stomach plunged, twisting into knots.

CHAPTER TWENTY

Ava stood and walked toward him, and Grits cleared his throat, struggling to find the right words. How could he explain that what happened couldn't happen again? They'd be sharing a bed, and his desire for her was so strong, he couldn't bear to let her get that close without touching her.

Before he could speak, she cut in smoothly, "Don't give me the 'it's not you, it's me' speech."

He was about to correct her, but she was already on a fiery roll.

"I know you confided a weakness in me, so don't worry, your secret's safe. But I told you I wouldn't regret it, and I don't. Not one bit, Grits. And if you're upset over that silly line, then you need a wake-up call."

He crossed his arms, a smile playing on his lips as she continued her passionate speech.

"You promised not to lie to me, so you'd better keep that promise. Now, do you still want me?"

He nodded, ready to respond, but she wasn't finished.

"Then I don't want to hear anything else. We'll tackle this together. You won't lose me, and you won't carry that guilt. You'll protect me, even if we're sharing a bed."

"Are you quite done?" A teasing smirk played on his lips.

She looked away, cheeks flushing with embarrassment, and he secretly reveled in the sight. She nodded, hesitant.

"Okay, I was going to tell you that what happened can't happen again." Before she could speak, he gently pressed a finger to her soft lips, silencing her. "I was going to say that, but Ava, I can't be near you without wanting to touch you. It still scares the hell out of me that I might be the reason something happens to you, but I can't let you go."

She kissed his finger softly, his fingertips lingering over her mouth as if sealing a secret.

"I want something between us, Ava." His voice trembled with longing. "But now isn't the time to dwell on what-ifs. Right now, I need to focus on the threat." He gently withdrew his hand, feeling the sting of absence.

"That's my job—to find the threat."

He shook his head, a hint of resolve in his eyes. "You're looking for the mastermind. I'm hunting for threats."

She gulped, her eyes searching his face. "Do you think they'll find us out here?"

He paused, pondering. It seemed unlikely, but his past was a tangled maze, and someone might dig into his history, check with his SEAL teammates. They wouldn't find Salty easily. Yet, he remained vigilant. "No."

She narrowed her eyes, the challenge clear. "You promised to be honest with me."

He chuckled softly, shaking his head. She was going

to hold that promise over him forever. That realization surprised him. Why did he think the rest of his life? He'd only just met her.

Yet, there was something deeper between them that transcended their physical intimacy. There was an unspoken bond that loomed larger and more profound than sex itself. They shared a connection built on mutual trust, a bond neither of them took lightly. He had confided in her with a heavy heart, revealing his fears for their safety, their relationship, and even their very lives. The weight of this secret was immense, and he wondered if she truly understood its significance.

From what he sensed, she did. Otherwise, she wouldn't have given him that heartfelt speech earlier, filled with reassurance and understanding.

He reached out to pull her close just as the door swung open, and Salty's familiar figure stepped inside.

Salty grinned. "All set, LT."

Grits groaned softly, letting the moment with Ava slip away. "Great. Hey, do you happen to have a sat phone?" Out here, cell phones were useless. Where would they even find bars? He figured Salty, ever prepared, kept a satellite phone for emergencies.

"Sure thing. Hang on, I'll get it." Salty headed off to his bedroom.

Grits stopped him. "I also need a full clip or two for a 9mm."

Salty nodded and continued on his way.

Grits seized the moment, swooping down to surprise Ava with a quick, playful kiss.

Her eyes widened in surprise. "What was that for?" A

hint of blush stained her cheeks.

"Just because you're you." He winked.

Salty returned, holding out a sat phone and two clips with a sly smile. "Here you go. Charged and ready to go." His old teammate hesitated for a moment, concern flickering in his eyes. "Are you sure it's wise?"

He wasn't entirely convinced himself, but he knew he had to check in and let Jesse know he was alive.

Grits reached out instinctively for the items, taking them from Salty's hand. "No, but it's necessary."

Salty nodded, his face calm but alert. "Got it."

Most likely, the man understood. The challenge wasn't tracking a satellite phone. It was harder than tracing a cell. Yet, with Salty, there was a good chance the GPS features were disabled, which would make it harder.

He glanced at his watch. It was two in the afternoon. "Salty—"

Salty interrupted with a quick nod. "I'm heading to rest."

Ava looked confused. "But—"

Grits cut her off before she could finish. "He needs to sleep so he can stay on watch tonight."

Ava nodded sharply. "Oh." Without hesitation, she turned on her heel and headed back to the computers.

He knew she relied heavily on Salty's expertise, but he was confident she would handle it. Her mission was clear: trace the origin of the encrypted message. That was their mastermind's signature. It likely pointed to some hacker, but with the right persuasion from HIS, they'd uncover who was truly behind it all.

Salty gave him a quick nod before heading to his

bedroom, leaving Grits standing there alone.

Anxiety gnawed at him. Was he dooming his friend and his woman with the call he was about to make? The weight of it pressed down, heavy with possibility and peril.

Before stepping out of the cabin, he reached down and carefully inserted a fresh magazine into the chamber of his firearm, which had been resting at his side. He then took the second magazine, ensuring it was securely placed in his pocket for quick access if needed.

He took a few cautious steps away, circling around to survey his surroundings. The silence was thick. There wasn't even a single critter stirring anywhere, not even a whisper in the woods.

He dialed the number he'd memorized by heart. He would call Jesse's personal cell, not the HIS hotline. The line rang, each second stretching longer than the last.

When Jesse finally answered, his voice was hesitant, almost wary. "Yeah?"

"How's Daylan?"

Jesse quickly muffled the phone, whispering to someone, "I have to take this. I'll be right back."

Grits caught the shift in Jesse's tone. His trust wasn't exactly flowing freely here, and that realization gave him a flicker of hope.

After a brief pause, Jesse returned to the call. "I'm sorry, Grits, but he didn't make it."

The words hit like a punch to the gut. Grits staggered, reaching out to steady himself against a nearby tree, feeling the weight of loss and the sharp sting of disappointment settle deep within.

He had just lost another man. That made four men who had lost their lives in his career. Four too many. Each loss weighed heavily on him, the emotional burden pressing down like an unbearable weight, leaving him feeling overwhelmed by grief and responsibility.

He never should have asked for help. If he'd kept quiet, Daylan might still be alive today. But if he'd handled it solo, Ava could have been caught in the drone attack instead—and that thought made his stomach churn. Every choice, every hesitation, felt like a weight on his shoulders now.

"What about Buddy?"

"He's fine and with Pup and Elena."

He braced himself, expecting Jesse to chide him for going dark without permission. But instead, Jesse's words caught him off guard. "Are you safe?"

He knew he couldn't stay on the line long. Quickly, he replied, "We are."

"Do you trust the guy the team pulled from Celeb's cabin?"

Thinking about the disaster he'd caused at his friend's cabin made him frown. "I do."

"Good. Stay dark."

Grits had already decided that no matter what Jesse said, he would stay off everyone's radar. Ava's safety depended on it, and so did exposing a dangerous secret.

"By the way, how's Devon coming along?"

"Slow," was the curt answer, leaving a heavy silence in the air.

"What about government contacts? Can't someone help with this?"

The reply was cold and cautious. "We don't know who to trust."

His mind raced. If they suspected someone in government, then the very best at hiding encrypted messages would be a cryptologist. Suddenly, they had a large pool of suspects, and trust became a rare commodity.

"How's Ava coming along with it?"

He mimicked Jesse's reply with, "Slow."

"If something happens, call me. Otherwise, I don't want to hear from you until you've figured this out."

The weight of those words pressed heavily on his shoulders, fueling his anxiety.

"And the leak?" He needed to know who the agent responsible for risking his life and Ava's was.

"I'm on it. Stay safe out there." With a sigh, Jesse ended the call, leaving a tense silence hanging in the air.

Grits turned the sat phone off with a frustrated sigh. This was a nightmare. Leaving Ava to shoulder such a heavy burden felt like an impossible task. She seemed to be managing the stress well, but he knew it was only a matter of time before it overwhelmed her. Living under constant threat was no easy task, yet she placed her unwavering trust in him.

And that was her mistake. He couldn't even protect a team of specially trained operatives. How could he possibly keep her safe? Salty's cabin was a perfect hideout, but he sensed their time was slipping away.

He couldn't identify any specific reason for this feeling. Perhaps it was the meticulous preparations Salty had made for them.

Salty. Was he wrong to involve Salty in this mess? By bringing him here, he had put his friend's life at risk. But where else could he find safety?

He pondered this, realizing that behind the HIS double doors lay sanctuary. Yet, he couldn't enter HIS without risking exposing Ava to danger.

While he carefully pondered their next move, he methodically retraced their egress route in his mind, visualizing every turn and potential obstacle. He was acutely aware that each misstep could be disastrous, perhaps even costing him a leg if he slipped or faltered. It was imperative that he memorize this escape route perfectly, as it was the only way to ensure Ava's swift safety.

He made a mental note to ask Salty about an alternate route, suspecting that, with his resourcefulness, Salty had a backup plan in place in case the primary path became compromised. There was no doubt in his mind that Salty's preparedness extended beyond what was obvious and that he'd have a contingency ready if needed.

When he reached the first vehicle, hidden beneath a camouflage cover, he paused for a moment, his heart pounding. Carefully, he pulled back the cover, revealing the go-bags inside. He checked them again. While Salty had weapons in the cabin, they'd need more firepower and ammunition to stay ahead on the run.

Confident that everything was in order, he quickly covered the truck with the camo again. He retraced his steps, found the route to the second vehicle, and moved swiftly through the woods, repeating the familiar routine. After securing that one as well, he began heading back toward the cabin.

Just as he was about one hundred yards away, a twig snapped loudly, piercing the tense silence.

CHAPTER TWENTY-ONE

Ava smiled as she gazed at the monitor, which displayed Grits. He was visibly on high alert, his eyes sharp and scanning the surroundings intently. Suddenly, her smile faded, and her heart lurched painfully in her chest when she saw Grits abruptly stop in his tracks. Without hesitation, he swiftly drew his gun, signaling that they had been discovered.

Frantically, Ava's eyes darted across the other monitors and the various squares within the system, searching desperately for any signs of the approaching danger. Just as she was on the verge of waking Salty to warn him, her gaze caught the image of Grits' foe. It was a large buck, tensing and slowly entering the area near him, its presence both alarming and oddly reassuring.

A wave of relief washed over her, and she couldn't help but laugh silently. After all, they hadn't been found yet.

Watching closely, she saw Grits calmly holster his weapon as he turned to face the buck. His expression was serious but composed, and his posture relaxed yet alert. She could see his lips moving, speaking in a low, steady voice, perhaps giving orders or making a reassuring comment. The buck listened intently, its head slightly tilted as if trying to understand or heed his words. She laughed softly to herself, entertained by the scene. She could only imagine what he was saying. It was probably something with a calm authority or a touch of humor to ease the tension between them.

Returning to her task with renewed focus, she carefully examined and sifted through the data, seeking to trace the elusive entity that had infiltrated the system and inserted the decrypted message. This action was far more critical than simply identifying who had breached the system, because the true danger lay in the fact that this entity was actively trying to kill her since she uncovered the message, making the threat to her life imminent and urgent.

As if that weren't enough to consider, she vividly recalled Grits sitting across from her during lunch, talking softly about his old teammates and the numerous losses they'd suffered over the years. They had skimmed over the details, brushing past the pain, but she could see each memory hit him hard, reflected in the somber look in his eyes. Based on what she knew of him so far, she was certain he held himself responsible for those deaths, carrying an unspoken guilt that weighed heavily on his shoulders.

How could she possibly help him? Was she truly the right person for this delicate task, or was she merely fooling herself? After a moment of reflection, she resolved that she was indeed the one. She would find a way, no matter the cost, to free his tormented soul from the crushing weight of guilt that relentlessly ate away at him, threatening to consume him entirely. She knew it wouldn't be easy, but her determination was unshakable.

As he turned away from the buck and headed back toward the cabin, she eagerly scanned the monitors once more, her mind racing with possibilities before returning to her task. The code had been masterfully embedded into the bank's system, and she couldn't shake the suspicion that this wasn't just a simple message to the Chinese.

She liked to believe it was merely the Chinese consulate exchanging information, but deep down, she knew better. They wouldn't be so obvious, and they certainly had diplomatic channels for passing messages. Something about this felt different and dangerously intriguing.

She scoffed at her thoughts. Dangerous, indeed. But honestly, nothing was more perilous than her current life. Realizing she was ill-equipped to face threats without Grits or Salty by her side, she made a quick decision that she'd ask them to teach her how to shoot a gun and fight, just enough to escape if she ever got captured.

A shiver ran down her spine at the thought. Shaking off the fear, she decided to focus on one thing—code. It was cold, calculated, and far removed from the chaos her life had become. It was a sanctuary where she could find clarity amidst the storm.

She wasn't quite sure how long she had been working at her computer when she suddenly felt a gentle touch on her shoulder. Turning slightly, she saw Grits standing nearby with a warm smile. "Sweetheart, it's time to take a break."

Despite feeling reluctant to stop, she knew that staying

focused was important, which meant she needed to step away from the screen periodically. Reluctantly, she sighed and slowly stood up, stretching her arms above her head to alleviate some of the strain from sitting so long. As she stretched, she let out a small yawn, feeling the fatigue catching up with her. Her eyes flicked to the clock on the wall. What time was it now? The room was quiet except for the faint hum of her computer and the distant sounds of the generator running the cabin.

Surprised to see Salty awake, and, based on his wet hair, recently showered, she stiffened. Her stomach clenched as her focus wavered, caught off guard by the sudden shock. She had to remain alert, and she'd lost herself in her computer code. What if her would-be killers decided to approach the cabin when Salty was asleep and Grits patrolled outside? Salty had mentioned his alarms would wake him if anything was wrong, yet she knew there were multiple unguarded entrances she hadn't seen or considered. The looming threat pressed heavily on her mind, demanding every ounce of her focus as she fought to steady her nerves.

"Ava? Sweetheart?" Grits' voice was gentle but insistent.

She looked up at him and offered a small, grateful smile. "Thank you. I really needed that break."

He studied her closely, a flicker of concern crossing his face.

She didn't want him to see her so upset. If he did, he'd never leave her side, and she couldn't have him underfoot while she was trying to focus on finding the source of that encrypted message.

"Okay." He nodded toward the kitchen. "Dinner's almost ready. I wasn't sure if you'd want to wash up first."

She realized she needed to splash cold water on her face. The scent of food and the warmth of the kitchen drifted around her, but she'd been so absorbed in her task that she hadn't even noticed. That wouldn't do. She needed to regain her composure, fast.

"I do. Thank you." She freed herself from the alcove where Salty had set up his large workstation and security monitors. She hurried into the one small bathroom, splashing cold water on her face, her reflection revealing dark circles beneath her eyes as proof of a restless night's sleep.

Both she and Grits had barely slept, and the toll was evident after a full day glued to the computer. She would claim they'd catch up on rest tonight, but deep down, she knew better. There was no way she'd let him crawl into her bed without being with him.

After using the facilities, she stepped into the living room, only to be greeted by the tempting aroma of pizza. Her eyes widened in surprise.

Sensing her curiosity, Salty raised his hand with a teasing smile. "Don't get too excited. It's just frozen."

But she didn't mind. Pizza was her comfort food, especially after realizing she'd nearly lost an entire day searching for the source.

As she savored a few slices, they chatted about Grits' discoveries throughout the day. She couldn't help but notice he avoided mentioning any conversations with a woodland animal, leaving her more intrigued than ever.

After shoving a mouthful of food in his mouth, Salty tried to speak but had to settle for chewing instead. With everyone's eyes fixed on him, they waited eagerly for him to continue.

"Maybe we're approaching this the wrong way."

Grits raised an eyebrow. "How so?"

Salty held up a hand. "Hear me out. Maybe finding the source is a task we'll never truly complete." He paused, then tilted his head. "Maybe we should trace the leak back from HIS and follow it upstream. Whoever's leaking probably has access somewhere, either listening in on conversations or slipping information from the system. I find it hard to believe this is their first attempt."

Grits considered this, then nodded slowly. "We've definitely had a few missions end up tit's-up."

Ava sputtered on her pizza at that statement, her eyes widening in surprise.

"Sorry." Grits grinned mischievously. "A few missions don't always go as planned."

She nodded, catching the hint the first time. Instead, she chose to focus on Salty's thoughts. "So, you're saying we should break into HIS's system and track the leak?" Anticipation tingled in her voice and gut.

Grits shook his head, a serious look replacing his grin. "I wouldn't count on it. Devon's got top-tier cybersecurity defenses."

"I'll find a way." Excitement bubbling inside her, she started to rise, eager to act.

But Grits gently placed a hand on her arm. "Tomorrow."

Disappointment crossed her face as she realized she'd

have to hold back, her mind already racing with plans to crack an unbreakable system.

Then, she and Salty huddled over a notebook, plotting their next move. After being left out for a while, Grits quietly collected their dishes, carried them to the sink, and washed away the remnants. She frowned, realizing there would be no cold pizza while working on her morning project.

Once they finished, Salty stepped outside for his usual reconnaissance, calling it a "look around."

Ava knew he was checking his booby traps, scanning the woods for any sign of danger.

She and Grits sat at the table drinking tea. Grits reached over and rubbed her tense shoulder. She nearly turned so he could massage both, but hesitated, worried it might seem too demanding.

"Grits?"

"Yeah, sweetheart?"

She appreciated how he used that name—soft, genuine, untainted by chauvinism. It made her feel cared for. Then, she took a deep breath, summoning courage. "I'd like you to teach me to shoot a gun."

His hand froze.

She pressed on. "And to fight."

"I don't think it's necessary, but if that's what you want…."

Even though he trailed off, she didn't care. He'd agreed. "Great. When can we start?"

The tension in the room thickened as they contemplated their next move, the weight of uncertainty pressing down, yet fueling her determination.

CHAPTER TWENTY-TWO

Grits dimmed the main lights, allowing only the soft glow from the bedside lamp to fill the room. As he undressed, each piece of clothing fell away, leaving him in just his underwear. His attention was drawn to Ava, who remained in her T-shirt and panties. Her simple yet captivating attire held Grits in a spell, his heart pounding and his thoughts momentarily lost in her enchanting presence.

As they nestled into bed, he reached out to her with a gesture that was both tender and urgent. "Now, we have much to discuss." He gently turned her to face him, their chests touching, feeling the warmth and rhythm of her breath against his skin. Her presence ignited a surge of excitement and a comforting sense of security within him.

"What's on your mind?"

"This," he breathed, his voice barely above a whisper, before sealing her lips with his own. The kiss began with a nearly brutal intensity, a passionate release of emotions that had been building throughout the night. It was a tormenting yet challenging embrace, a testament to his desire to keep her safe, yet his unwillingness to let her go once the threat was over.

His kiss was a dance of contradictions, fierce and tender, as his tongue continued its relentless exploration, while his lips softened, allowing the kiss to gently deepen. It was a moment of vulnerability and connection, where time seemed to stand still, and the world outside faded away, leaving only the two of them in their intimate cocoon.

When her breath caught, he lifted his head a fraction, his gaze lingering on her exquisite beauty as she entered the prelude to passion. Her eyes, dark and mysterious, seemed to hold the universe within them, while her cheeks were flushed with a delicate pink hue, adding to her allure. Her breaths came in ragged, uneven patterns, each one a testament to the intensity of the moment.

He couldn't resist the irresistible pull of her swollen lips, which seemed to beckon him closer. He brushed them gently, savoring the softness and warmth, then twice more, each touch more tender than the last. Finally, he covered her mouth with a soft, loving kiss, pouring all his emotions of care, desire, and love into it. The kiss was a silent promise, a deep connection that spoke volumes of his affection and longing for her.

Suddenly, a wave of urgency surged through him. "I have to have you."

Her response was immediate and unwavering, "I'm yours."

He paused, contemplating the weight of her words. Did she truly understand the implications of what she had just said? He yearned for her to be his, not just for the immediate purpose of ensuring her safety, but for a much longer, enduring future together.

As she slipped off her T-shirt, he couldn't help but admire her stunning breasts. Gently cradling one in his hand, he marveled at its softness and traced his thumb over her nipple, drawing a tender moan from her lips.

"Shh."

Her eyes, heavy with desire, met his, filled with a yearning that spoke volumes. "Sorry. That just feels good."

A smile played on his lips. "So you like this. Do you?"

"Mm hmm," she murmured, her lips glistening with anticipation. "Are you going to kiss me again?"

This woman was the very essence of temptation, blissfully unaware of her allure.

"I just might." His lips grazed her delicate skin before descending down her smooth throat to her breast. As he gently took her nipple into his mouth, he placed a hand over her lips to muffle her moans, ensuring Salty remained blissfully ignorant.

The seasoned veteran knew exactly what they were doing, but he also understood that Ava would be mortified if their passion was laid bare for Salty to hear.

After a brief pause, he resumed his journey down her smooth, silky skin, tracing a path over her stomach and moving closer to her core. Removing her panties, he inhaled her intoxicating scent, a wave of overwhelming desire washed over him, making him feel as though he might come right then and there. He had longed to taste her before, to savor the sweetness of her essence, but his overwhelming eagerness to be inside her had taken precedence, leaving him no time to indulge in such pleasures.

She squirmed and moved her legs with increasing intensity as he gently licked her wet center, her body responding eagerly to his touch. Her soft moans and gasps filled the room, signaling to him that she was enjoying the experience just as much as he was.

Lifting his head slightly to observe her reactions, he carefully inserted a finger inside her, feeling the warmth and softness of her body. He then added a second finger, mimicking the rhythm and motion of lovemaking, eliciting more passionate responses from her. Her body arched towards him, and her breathing quickened.

Ava reached down, her fingers gently grasping his shoulders, her eyes locked with his, an intensity that made his heart race. "Now."

Her soft command left him breathless and unable to refuse. Who was he to argue with the woman who lay naked beside him, her skin warm and inviting? He turned his gaze to the nightstand, where he had placed a condom earlier, a small token of gratitude to Salty for always keeping them stocked for other uses. Carefully, he opened the package, rolled it onto himself, ensuring it was secure.

With a deep breath, he positioned himself over her, feeling the soft curve of her thighs beneath him. As he leaned forward, his forehead resting gently against hers, he moved slowly, each stroke deliberate and tender, feeling her body respond to him. He continued to deepen each thrust, savoring the connection between them, until he was fully seated, feeling the warmth and closeness that enveloped him.

Euphoria surged through his veins, electrifying his nerve endings with every movement inside her. Their lovemaking began with a gentle rhythm, each tender stroke drawing him nearer to the edge. As her fingertips dug into his shoulders, he sensed her nearing climax, and he focused on his strokes, resisting the urge to go hard and heavy.

"Faster."

Her soft whisper seemed to spark a blazing fire within him, igniting an intense passion that consumed them both. Their lovemaking quickly escalated into a frenzied and rapid dance of desire, each movement fueled by an overwhelming need for one another. He was grateful they didn't have a spring mattress beneath them, so that Salty, in the next room, couldn't hear the fervent rhythm of their lovemaking.

As the intensity built, he felt a powerful surge of sensation coursing through him, starting at the base of his spine and tightening his every muscle. His breath came in ragged gasps as he leaned in, capturing her lips with his own. In that moment, she cried out his name, her voice a melody of ecstasy that resonated deep within his chest. Overwhelmed by the sheer force of his emotions, he let go, releasing a deep, guttural groan that echoed the culmination of their shared passion.

After catching his breath, he gently rolled off Ava, feeling the warmth of their connection linger. He stood up, casually tossing the condom into the garbage can beside the bed. With a contented sigh, he lay back down beside her, pulling her close. They nestled into each other's arms, the soft tremors in his limbs a lingering reminder of the passion they had just shared.

It would be so easy to fall for this woman. He'd

already let her in more than any other woman in his life. That had to mean something. But was it something akin to love? He scoffed at the idea. He couldn't love her this quickly. It was the adrenaline of their circumstance. But, deep down, he knew differently.

"You kept your promise."

Confused for a moment, he turned to her. "What?"

She smiled, and his heart lit up with something he couldn't quite understand. "You promised to make me say your name when I came."

He smiled, pride swelling within him as he remembered her mouthing his name against his lips. "Glad to be of service."

She laughed. As she traced her hand gently up and down his chest, a soft smile played on her lips. "Was there something you wanted to talk about, or was that it?"

He hesitated, not wanting to upset her, but he knew honesty was best. Holding her close, he took a deep breath. "It's about Daylan."

Her expression shifted instantly, worry clouding her features. "Oh my gosh, I forgot to ask—how is he?"

The concern in her voice was unmistakable, and he hated to be the bearer of bad news, but it had to come out. He pulled her closer, his voice breaking. "I'm sorry, sweetheart. He didn't make it."

Her breath hitched as her hand darted to her mouth, trembling. "No. Please tell me it isn't true." Her voice was barely a whisper, full of disbelief and fear.

He hesitated, his jaw clenched. "I wish I could, but I promised I wouldn't lie to you."

Tears welled up in her eyes. "He died protecting me."

Her voice cracked.

No one knew better than him the pain of losing someone around you, especially someone who was putting their life on the line for yours. His own heart had borne that burden—teammates in SEALs bound by unbreakable trust, each ready to lay down their lives for the others. And yet, he had failed them. He hadn't been enough.

But he couldn't let her drown in that grief, in that guilt. The same heavy guilt that had haunted him since he'd heard of Daylan's death. The man had been in his command, and he'd failed him. Just like he'd failed his teammates. He swallowed hard, fighting to keep his emotions in check, knowing that the weight of loss was a heavy burden they both carried.

He gently embraced her, holding her close as she wept uncontrollably, her sobs echoing through the room.

She pounded her tiny fist against his chest. Her voice was filled with grief. "He died protecting me. Why? Why did it have to happen?"

The raw pain in her voice cut through the air, resonating deeply within his chaotic mind. He understood she wasn't looking for words or answers. She simply needed to be held in that moment of vulnerability, so he held her tight, offering silent comfort amidst the turmoil.

Her tears flowed freely, leaving her face flushed and her breathing labored from the congestion in her nose. Anticipating this emotional moment, he had thoughtfully prepared by placing a box of tissues conveniently on the nightstand, ready to offer comfort.

As he observed her tenderly blowing her nose, he

noticed the blush of embarrassment that spread across her cheeks. This small, vulnerable gesture filled him with renewed hope.

"I'm sorry, Grits. I know he was your teammate."

He had doubted him before, a mistake he now regretted. Despite his flaws, the man had been dependable and willing to risk everything, even his life, to protect Ava. He gently rubbed her arm, trying to offer comfort amid the chaos. "We'll get through this, sweetheart."

Her eyes searched his face, seeking answers. "Why didn't you tell me earlier?"

He hesitated, knowing the truth would hit hard. "Because I knew you'd want to grieve in private."

Silence fell between them, thick with unspoken emotion. Finally, she sighed deeply, her shoulders relaxing just a bit. "You were right."

Gently cupping her cheek, he leaned in to kiss her softly. He imagined she'd have more tears for Daylan and the reason for his loss, but now, she was ready for the next level of his plan.

"Was there anything else?"

"Yes. Tomorrow, we practice our escape."

CHAPTER TWENTY-THREE

Grits' mouth moved over Ava's with the care of an expert lover, each kiss a tantalizing blend of skill and sensual grace. His lips brushed hers softly, then his tongue slipped in smoothly, exploring her with confident, deliberate strokes that ignited a fire beneath her skin. Ava couldn't imagine waking up without this electric intimacy, craving it every single morning.

When he broke the kiss and whispered, "It's time to wake up, sweetheart," she groaned in playful protest. But then, a thrilling realization struck her that today was the day she would attempt to crack the impenetrable HIS system. Her heart raced with excitement at the challenge, and she nearly leaped from his arms, ready to conquer the day.

He chuckled, his hand gliding up and down her back. "Settle down. You've got time."

She was torn between the allure of Grits and the adrenaline of her mission. They could indulge in passion anytime, but his kiss had ignited a fire within her. Yet, the thought of breaking into the HIS system was equally exhilarating. She wanted to squeal with joy at both possibilities.

Grits decided for her. "I've been up for hours, and I've already relieved Salty. I thought you might want to get up since it's pushing nearly ten o'clock."

She shot upright, heart pounding. "Ten o'clock!" How had she slept so deeply? Suddenly, she recalled their conversation about Daylan's death last night. Tears welled in her eyes at the thought of him losing his life because of her. Then, Grits had agreed to train her. Finally, he'd held her close, making slow, passionate love to her again for hours.

Grits must've seen the tears threatening to spill over in her eyes.

"It's going to be okay, sweetheart. I'm not telling you to forget, but you have to compartmentalize Daylan's news. You can't let it derail you from finding his killer."

That hadn't occurred to her. That she'd also find the man responsible for Daylan's murder. A surge of renewed determination flooded her veins at the thought of finally reaching that goal.

Ava wiped her eyes, took a deep breath, and nodded. "I'm ready." She could compartmentalize like the best of them, especially once she immersed herself in her computer coding.

Throwing off the covers with a confident flair, she stood up, completely unfazed by her bareness, and reached for her bag, wishing they had an en-suite for a quick freshen-up before getting dressed. Instead, she swiftly slipped into her clothes and was swept into Grits' embrace.

"I've got to dive back into my task, but we'll tackle training later today." His voice was a playful whisper.

With a mischievous grin, he leaned down, planting a quick kiss on her lips before giving her a gentle slap on the butt.

"Hey!" She rubbed her butt cheek with a smile. She adored this playful side of him.

They stepped out of the bedroom into the stillness of the quiet cabin. She guessed Salty was probably asleep, preparing to cover night duty once again. She couldn't help but miss the grizzly man sitting at the computer with his endless flow of knowledge and ideas. He'd been a fountain of inspiration, especially for the one she was about to try.

After a quick freshen-up in the cabin's bathroom, Ava dashed toward the computer bank, eager to get started, only to be halted by Grits.

"Breakfast first." He pulled out a chair and settled at the table. Her eyes were drawn to the plate of eggs and sausage waiting for her, along with the signature bowl of grits. She almost snorted with amusement at the small yet persistent routines amid the chaos of her life.

She settled at the small table, anticipation buzzing in her chest as she prepared to eat. The warm, nourishing meal did more than satisfy her hunger. It ignited a fire within, energizing her both physically and mentally and sharpening her focus. A wave of confidence and determination washed over her, bridging the gap between her nerves and readiness. This wasn't just any daunting task. It was a high-stakes operation of breaking into a highly secure system. The thought of potentially pulling it off sent a thrill down her spine, making her giddy at the prospect of an exhilarating victory.

"Do you really think you can pull it off?"

Ava's playful smirk tugged at her lips as she took a deliberate bite of her toast, generously spread with strawberry jelly. She paused, savoring the sweet tartness as she contemplated her answer. After swallowing, she offered a confident, teasing smile. "I don't know for sure, but I'm definitely going to give it my all."

Grits' face lit up with pride, a broad smile spreading across his face. "That's my girl." His eyes shone with admiration.

Her heart fluttered at the affectionate praise, a surge of warmth and pride swelling within her as he called her "his girl."

After breakfast, Grits confidently announced he'd take charge of the dishes, giving her the perfect excuse to dive into her work. Without hesitating, her fingers danced across the keyboard, hunting for just the right code to crack into HIS and knowing full well it wouldn't be easy, but relishing the thrill of the challenge.

When Salty brought up the mission, it sounded almost impossible, yet a spark of curiosity ignited within her. It made perfect sense that the leak had come from someone with access, and most likely someone within HIS. Given that they used individual logins, tracking the intruder should be straightforward. Grits' instincts pointed to a member of Charlie team, especially since this appeared to be a fresh connection, and he knew the other team members well.

He kept mentioning someone named Justin Franks, brother to the second-in-command on Alpha team. Justin previously worked for a notorious worldwide drug dealer, albeit to find his father's killer, but Grits wasn't ready to trust him as easily as he trusted the Hamilton brothers.

She knew the path to the HIS system was straightforward, but breaking into it was another story altogether. Lost in her own world, she poured every ounce of her knowledge into hacking her way in. The day before, she had started with reconnaissance, grilling Grits about the system's infrastructure and its vulnerabilities. Unfortunately, his answers didn't shed much light, so this morning, she pushed further, probing to see what she was truly up against.

Her fingers continued their dance over her keyboard as she scanned for open ports, network services, and subtle weaknesses, with each discovery a secret waiting to be uncovered. Every closed door she encountered, she skillfully opened a new one, fueled by determination.

When no obvious entry point remained, her last resort would be to plant a malicious bug that Salty had said he'd created. It was something that could wreak havoc on HIS. But that wasn't her style. She envisioned slipping in unseen, slipping out just as quietly, leaving no trace behind. An invisible ghost in the system.

She started by fiddling with Grits' login and password, trying to find a gateway. His access granted her a lot of data, but it was mostly useless to her. Her progress was cut short by security clearances that simply wouldn't let her go further, bouncing her back each time she tried to breach new areas.

Undeterred, she attempted a daring remote code execution, hoping to breach the targeted server. She pushed further than before, gaining ground she never thought possible. Until she was abruptly shut down.

A creeping sensation nagged at her that someone was watching, tracking her movements and blocking her every move when she neared something important, like an unseen guardian in the shadows.

If that were the case, the stakes had just gotten higher, and the game had become more dangerous.

She jumped, her heart racing as someone suddenly touched her shoulders. Lost once again in the world of code, she'd momentarily forgotten her surroundings. But when she recognized the familiar, soothing touch of her lover, she relaxed, a gentle smile spreading across her face.

"How's it coming?" He kneaded her tense shoulders, and she couldn't help but moan in pleasure.

Shaking her head, she reached for a soda nearby, now warm from neglect. "Nothing yet." She couldn't hide the frustration in her voice.

"It's early. You'll get there."

His unwavering confidence was like music to her ears, renewing her hope. He trusted her with a monumental task. It was a challenge that made her wonder if she was truly up to it.

"It's time for a break and something to eat."

She glanced at the clock on her computer. Nearly three in the afternoon. She stretched her neck from side to side as Grits moved away, giving her the space she needed. Straightening her spine, she grasped the chair arms, using them to support her weight as she loosened the tension that had been building there. The relief was instant.

They settled into their usual lunchtime routine,

munching on sandwiches. Grit had promised a feast for dinner, featuring chicken, potatoes, and corn, along with warm, buttery cornbread, which was her absolute favorite. The anticipation made her smile, as she already looked forward to what was to come.

Salty joined them as they finished their meal. They settled quietly as he ate. Her fingers itched to dive back into the keyboard, but her mind was focused on picking his brain. She carefully explained all her progress and eagerly sought his advice.

He took a slow bite, furrowing his brow in thought. "Have you tried a SQL injection?"

No, she hadn't. The thought of injecting malicious SQL commands into the website's input fields—potentially dumping the entire database—should have been among her first tactics. How had she overlooked it?

A surge of excitement drove her to jump up from the table, rushing back to her computer. Her hands darted over the keyboard, ready to test her next move, energized by the challenge.

Before her full attention was glued to the computer screen, she suddenly heard Grits chuckle—a low, knowing sound that made her spine tingle.

After nearly two tense hours, she finally broke through. Yes, she was in! However, a twist awaited: her access was limited to specific databases. To unlock everything, she needed Devon's login and password because Grits had claimed he was the architect.

Her eyes lit up when she saw the password database. Smiling to herself, she began hashing, attempting to reverse the encryption and uncover the original passwords.

Amidst the hacking earlier—when she thought someone was fighting her on the other end—this task suddenly felt surprisingly easy. At last, she had what she needed to move forward.

"I'm in!" Her heart pounded as she turned around. The cabin was eerily silent, and a chill ran down her spine. Was everyone really gone? Fear prickled at her skin, imagining they'd leave her all alone. But then, her eyes caught the monitors. Grits was outside, his figure moving purposefully across the landscape, searching intently. Listening closely, she realized Salty was in the shower. Relief washed over her. She wasn't truly alone. They'd just stepped back, giving her space to focus.

Driven by curiosity, she began searching for her name, certain they had her file tucked away somewhere. Grits was protecting her, so they'd have done a quick workup on her. She scribbled down the names of those who'd accessed her file. Where should she look next? The mystery deepened, and she knew her next move could change everything.

It suddenly struck her how easily they'd uncovered Celeb's cabin. Curiosity overriding caution, she decided to dig into Grit's file. Although guilt tugged at her, she reasoned he must have had connections or known someone there. If Celeb's name appeared, she'd finally uncover who had recently accessed the file. Her heart pounding, she glanced at the door, feeling like she was crossing a line that was more than just hacking. With a deep breath, she accessed Grit's file. It'd had three recent visitors, and Celeb was listed as a friend. She quickly jotted down the names, comparing the lists with growing anticipation. Without thinking, she leapt from her chair and flung open the front door. Before Grit could say a word, she blurted out, "I know who the leak is!"

CHAPTER TWENTY-FOUR

Grits froze suddenly, his heart pounding fiercely in his chest. She'd cracked the case. Relief flooded him, mingling with a sharp surge of anger. Someone from the HIS circle had orchestrated the hit on Ava. That was utterly unacceptable.

He braced himself, expecting her to name Justin Franks. He was ready for the inevitable. But then, she surprised him.

"It's Joe Stone." A proud smile spread across her face as if revealing a hard-won victory.

His gut twisted in a knot of suspicion. "Are you certain?" She must've noticed his strained voice.

She nodded confidently. "It makes sense. He's the only one who accessed both of our files recently. Well, besides Devon."

He frowned, skeptical. "But Joe's Devon's right-hand man. Surely, he'd be combing through our files more often."

She took a deep breath, determined. "That's what I thought too. But then I traced his trail. He was digging into your file, looking for anyone connected to you. And Celeb was one of them."

Shock coursed through him. He couldn't believe the man he'd trusted so deeply was secretly working to end Ava's life. What had corrupted the man he thought he knew? Joe Stone had once been an FBI agent, starting out on a single team before shifting to cyber work alongside Devon. It had been his element.

But now? A traitor? That's what he was if he collaborated with those who planted that malicious code in the breach for the Chinese. They still didn't know the full message, but they were certain someone involved had a hand in it.

He scrubbed his weary face with his hand, the weight of the revelation pressing down. Now that they had a piece of the puzzle, how could they lure him out and uncover the mastermind behind it all? Grits was sure of one thing: Stone wasn't the kingpin of this operation. Whoever was pulling the strings remained hidden, and time was running out.

The tension in the air was palpable as he realized the spotlight would turn toward his former SEAL teammates. "It's time to practice our exit."

Ava looked at him, confusion etched on her face. "Didn't you hear? I found your leak."

He nodded, acknowledging her discovery. "I know. I'm just not sure what to do with it at the moment. So, let's practice getting the hell out of here if they find us."

Grits noticed the flicker of fear in Ava's eyes and felt a pang of guilt. He hadn't intended to frighten her. He only wanted to ensure she was ready. Gently closing the gap between them, he ran his hands up and down her arms in a comforting gesture. "It's okay. We just need to practice.

It's late today, so we'll practice shooting tomorrow." If they were there tomorrow.

He planned to inform Jesse about Ava's discovery, confident they would apprehend Stone, but he knew Ava wouldn't be safe until the mastermind was captured and neutralized.

She nodded, but he could sense her heart wasn't truly in it. Yet, it didn't matter. She needed to navigate the darkness if necessary, and with dusk descending, the moment was just right.

"Okay." Her determination was admirable, and he couldn't have been prouder.

He leaned in, capturing her lips with a precision that left no room for doubt. As she parted her lips, inviting him in, he felt a rush of exhilaration. Kissing her was intoxicating. With other women, it might lead to more, but with Ava, his thoughts were consumed by the possibilities that lay ahead.

Her warm lips were soft against his, and he applied a gentle pressure, yearning to claim her mouth and mark her as his own.

Salty cleared his throat behind them, cutting through the moment like a sharp knife. Grits itched to punch the man, but he held back. As he pulled away from the kiss, a grin spread across his face like a kid caught with his hand in the cookie jar.

"What was all the fuss about? Did you find out anything, Ava?"

Ava's eyes sparkled with excitement as she turned to him. "I found the leak."

Salty's face lit up with pride. "I knew you could do it."

He reached out and pulled Ava into a warm hug, prompting a low growl from Grits.

They both laughed, whether at the scene or Grit's playful reaction. He couldn't care less. No one was touching his woman.

Salty ran a hand through his damp hair, his eyes sharp with focus. "What's the next move, LT?"

"I need to make a call first. Then we practice getting the hell out of here."

Salty's grin widened, determination flashing in his eyes. "Will do."

Ava turned back, concern etched on her face. "Are you calling Jesse now?"

Grits nodded firmly. "The sooner we have Stone, the sooner this nightmare ends."

A flicker of hope crossed Ava's face. "Wouldn't that make us safe, then?"

He shook his head, a shadow passing over his features. "No. Someone else is involved, and they might already know everything Stone does."

Salty agreed to stay behind and prepare dinner, while Grits hurriedly ran Ava through their escape route one last time. A cold chill ran down his spine. He knew their window of safety was shrinking. It was crucial that Ava knew how to get out if something went wrong with Salty or him.

He shuddered at the thought of her being alone and on the run, and he vowed to do everything in his power to prevent that nightmare.

Before they could even begin their practice, he was faced with the hardest task of all—a call he dreaded more than anything. His stomach tightened in dread as he faced the brutal truth that he was about to betray one of their own. Desperately, he hoped against hope that their suspicions were wrong.

He headed inside to grab the satellite phone, his heartbeat pounding in his ears, and hurried back to the front yard. The weight of the moment bore down on him as he steadied his trembling hand and dialed the number, each ring stretching into an eternity until Jesse picked up his personal cell.

"Your girl is good." Jesse's voice was calm, yet it hinted at admiration.

A surge of pride rushed through Grits, fueling his confidence. Until Jesse's next words struck him like a blow.

"Not good enough. Devon caught on and cut her access."

A web of tension wrapped around him, tightening every second. Devon never missed a thing.

"He caught her logging in as him and followed her trail. We're probably on the same page."

There was a pause before Grits said one word. "Stone."

"Yeah, that bastard. We sent Alpha team after him, but he's in the wind."

His mind raced. Alpha team was back in the game. "And Bravo?"

"They're still on an op."

Well, he'd have Alpha team to rely on when the time came. But did he need them right now? No. Revealing their location could set off something Stone might find, and they were better off staying hidden.

"Stay dark until further notice." Jesse's commanding voice cut through the tension, signaling that this was far from over.

"Copy." Grits ended the call and powered down the sat phone.

Of all people, Stone was the last person he expected. The man had an estranged wife and kids, whom he saw every other weekend. What had changed to turn him into a traitor?

The call pushed from his mind, and he and Ava began their practice.

"Just past this gnarled tree," he whispered, his voice steady despite the tension, "you turn left and head straight for the hidden truck."

She paused, eyes scanning the surroundings as if engraving the scene into her memory, then nodded fiercely. "Okay. Once I get to the truck, what's next?"

Seeing her willingness to help, he decided to give her a task. "Help us uncover the truck." It would only take two of them to pull back the camo netting, but keeping her busy would ease her nerves.

Without hesitation, she turned left, leading him towards the truck, her steps quick and determined.

After Grits was confident Ava could navigate the woods to reach the first truck, he chose to wait until the next day for more practice. Darkness was creeping in, and without NVGs, navigation was challenging. Difficult but not impossible.

Back at the cabin, they gathered around the table for dinner with Salty, plotting their next move. The stakes were high, but their knowledge was limited. Two things were clear: first, the message was meant for the Chinese, and regardless of its content, it spelled bad news for the U.S. Second, Stone couldn't have acted alone. With these truths hanging in the air, every decision felt like walking a tightrope.

Salty shook his head, a hint of doubt clouding his eyes. "Our chances of decrypting that message are slim."

Ava nodded in agreement, her expression grim but hopeful.

Grits paused with his fork mid-air, curiosity flickering across his face. "But not impossible?"

Salty's slow nod reaffirmed his cautious optimism. "Not impossible."

Grits took a bite, then leaned back, pondering the weight of their quest. A flicker of frustration ran through him. He swallowed past the lump in his throat. "But what about pinpointing where the message was input? Who put it there? If we could find that, maybe it's our lead." His voice was tinged with fatigue but driven by determination.

"We might be able to trace where that message came from." Ava sighed, a hint of hope flickering in her voice. "But honestly, I'd bet my last dollar it's a hacker and not the original source."

Grits' jaw clenched in frustration. "That only takes us so far." His mind was already racing. HIS had to locate Stone and obtain the necessary intel. Meanwhile, Ava deserved better than this life of hiding, always looking over her shoulder, worried about the next egress route.

"Tomorrow's a brand new day. You can start fresh

then." Grits rose from the table and headed to the sink with his plate.

Salty appeared behind him, offering a reassuring smile. "I've got the dishes. You two go ahead and call it a night."

Grits didn't need to be told twice. Any chance to have Ava all to himself was a treasure he would seize. Especially if it meant wrapping her in his arms.

Together, he and Ava slipped into the bedroom, closing the door behind them. Anticipation buzzed in the air as he imagined her waiting for him, bare and beautiful on the bed.

He enveloped her in a warm embrace, holding her close. "How are you holding up?" He planted a gentle kiss on the top of her head.

"I'm fine. Just tired." Her voice was barely above a whisper.

A day glued to a computer screen had surely drained her mentally, and the run-through of their route had likely left her physically worn out as well.

"Let's just rest tonight." His heart ached at the thought of not being able to make love to her. But he knew she needed to be at her best, just in case their time at this hideout ran out. "In fact, let's keep our clothes on." He knew sleeping naked was a risk they shouldn't take, but he'd not been able to do anything other than with her the last few nights.

She pulled back, a flicker of fear in her eyes. "Are you expecting trouble?"

He shook his head reassuringly. "No, but if you're naked, I'd never be able to keep my hands from your body."

Her laughter rang out, a melody that struck his heart like the sweetest birdsong.

As they kicked off their shoes, the alarms tripped, and a siren sounded in the cabin.

They'd been found.

CHAPTER TWENTY-FIVE

Grits' heart pounded like a drum as the sound of pounding grew louder, sending a surge of adrenaline through his veins. He knew their time had been slipping away faster than he had hoped, and with Stone on the loose, he realized it had only been a matter of time before they discovered Salty's hideout.

"Get your shoes on." His command was sharper than intended, but urgency demanded it.

He watched her tremble as she slipped back into her tennis shoes, a pang of empathy tugging at him. He longed to comfort her…to hold her close, but duty held him back.

Instead, he focused on retying his boots, moving to the computer setup to do so. The video screens revealed the threat they faced, and he needed to be ready.

Salty entered the cabin, heading straight for his room. Grits knew what was coming. Salty was about to arm himself for the impending escape.

He spotted two teams, each with roughly six men, crossing Salty's property line. Suddenly, one man triggered a booby trap and went down. As the others approached from the opposite direction of their escape route, his pulse slowed, easing the tension in his mind and allowing him to think clearly.

After tying his boots, Salty reentered the living area. He handed Grits a pair of NVGs, a comm system, and an assault rifle. The men exchanged silent nods, an unspoken language forged through countless missions, trusting each other's instincts without a word.

Grits turned to Ava. "Are you ready?"

She nodded, fierce determination etched on her face, and he couldn't be prouder. Though fear flickered in her eyes, she stood prepared to run when the moment called for it.

Salty quickly fired up a program on the computer that Grits knew would wipe the system clean, erasing all traces of their keystrokes and activities. The moment he finished, they moved silently to the door, each step deliberate and practiced.

Initially, Salty was ready to set the cabin ablaze, but Grits quickly reminded him of the dangers. Those things could spiral out of control and spark a raging wildfire. They couldn't find safety if running through smoke, and the woodland creatures certainly didn't deserve to suffer from their actions. So, Salty had settled for wiping the computer memory.

As they exited the cabin, Salty took the lead, with Ava steady in the middle and Grits bringing up the rear. Grits had hoped to lead, but Salty's reasoning was clear that if they had to change course, he knew the shortcuts. Grits silently hoped they wouldn't need to divert from their planned route. Ava, familiar with the path, was the least likely to be spooked, and knowing what to expect should help keep her calm amid the tension.

With swift, silent steps, they maneuvered through the woods, turning left at the designated tree with practiced ease. Ava, ever the resilient trooper, kept pace behind Salty, while Grits fell back slightly to watch their six. Time was tight. They needed a few extra minutes upon arrival to strip the camo netting and get the truck running, so they couldn't have any unexpected surprises.

With his senses heightened, he froze momentarily to listen, but only the silence greeted him. There was no sign of them nearby. Instinct guiding him, he jogged closer to Ava, ensuring she was steadfastly following Salty and staying on the narrow, shadowy path.

Halfway to their destination, he slowed and dropped back again, ears tuned to the quiet. Faintly, he could hear the men as they discovered the empty cabin, then silence returned, deep and unbroken, along their route.

Just as he was about to move, a faint noise broke the stillness. His breath hitched. It might've been a deer, but he doubted it. Someone—or something—was nearby, possibly a team that had escaped their camera footage. He could feel their unspoken presence watching.

Ava and Salty needed time, so he quietly drifted back, ready to serve as a decoy if necessary. They had already devised a backup plan where Salty would proceed as planned, then drive Ava to a different rendezvous point where they would regroup.

Grits hunched in his crouch and slowed his breathing, his NVGs slicing through the darkness as he scanned the silent terrain. The eerie stillness was misleading. He knew the noise he'd heard wasn't a figment of his imagination.

Yet now, everything was unnaturally quiet. He stayed poised, muscles tensed, ready to pounce at any movement. But still, nothing emerged.

Convincing himself it was just a woodland creature, he relaxed slightly, rationalizing that the team couldn't have caught up yet.

He rose carefully, his steps deliberate as he followed the faint trail. Turning right at the next marker, he spotted Ava ahead, silently trailing behind Salty. She never looked back, just as he'd taught her. He'd explained the importance of his dropping back occasionally, so she wouldn't see him without NVGs that only he and Salty wore. Plus, he showed her how turning her head could cost precious seconds.

She'd understood, yet her frustration was evident at not keeping a constant eye on him. Still, he reassured her that he'd be at the egress point, on time, just as planned.

He still couldn't believe that Joe Stone, a man he once admired, was responsible for the chaos suddenly engulfing his and Ava's lives. The reasons behind Joe's actions remained a mystery, fueling his determination to uncover the truth at any cost. All Grits had ever heard about Joe was that he was an outstanding FBI agent, renowned for his sharp skills and unwavering dedication. Before stepping into a behind-the-scenes role in the computer division, Joe had built an impressive reputation as a sterling agent, earning colleagues' respect and admiration for his intelligence and integrity.

And now, this. His traitorous behavior was shocking, especially given his connection to the encrypted message involved in the data breach. The betrayal cut deep, and the need for answers grew more urgent with each passing moment.

Dropping back for one more pause, he froze, controlling his heavy breathing as he listened to the stillness of the woods. Though silent, a shiver ran down his spine, and the hairs on the back of his neck stood tall. Someone was near, whether they knew it or not. But he couldn't spot them yet.

He softly whispered over his comm, "Continue to point Bravo." He planned to meet them later. He wasn't about to join the others while their six wasn't covered.

Salty responded with two quick clicks on his mic, solid and sure.

Grits hadn't told Ava he might not make the rendezvous point. He silently hoped Salty wouldn't have a problem getting her to leave without him, knowing the mission's stakes. Every second counted in this game of shadows.

In the heart of the shadowy woods, he finally spotted a solitary figure. His finger hovered over the trigger, torn between hesitation and urgency. Who else would be wandering these woods under the cloak of night? As the man, also equipped with night vision goggles, caught sight of the trail, Grits pulled the trigger just as the truck engine coughed to life.

He knew the sound of gunfire would summon the others, so he sprinted in the opposite direction, determined to draw them away from Ava. Her safety was paramount, even if it meant sacrificing himself.

Pausing to scan the area, a chilling realization struck him. He hadn't heard the truck drive away. His heart pounded in his chest as he retraced his steps, praying he wasn't too late to rescue Ava and Salty. Fortunately, the silence was unbroken by gunfire.

As he approached the truck, he halted abruptly, his heart dropping into his stomach with a sickening lurch. The vehicle was encircled by a group of men clad in black, each brandishing assault rifles with a menacing presence.

Immediately, their eyes locked onto him. Without a second thought, they aimed straight for his chest. He gripped his assault rifle tightly, finger hovering on the trigger, every muscle tensed as he meticulously scanned their faces for any flicker of hesitation or signs of a sudden move.

One of these men aimed a flashlight directly at him, the beam piercing the darkness and momentarily blinding Grits, causing him to flinch and groan in discomfort. With a resigned sigh, he removed his night vision goggles, still feeling the harsh glare of the light on his face.

Inside the truck, Salty sat with his hands raised in a gesture of surrender, a gun pressed firmly against his temple. The men held Ava in a tight grip, her body tense with fear and defiance. She struggled against their hold, and Grits thought he saw her attempt to bite her captor, though he couldn't be certain in the dim light and chaos of the moment.

He knew Salty hadn't had a real chance. Otherwise, the men wouldn't have taken Ava. Salty would've given his life to save her, but in his current predicament, he could only give his life and still fail. So, he did what was right. If they survived this ordeal, they would rescue her.

And he'd make damn sure they all made it out alive, especially from the mercenaries.

Joe Stone slipped away from the group, voice sharp and commanding. "Don't even try it, Grits. You're surrounded."

Turning slowly, he realized they'd sneaked up behind him, silent as shadows. Fuck. Fuck. Fuck. He was screwed.

His voice, rough and unyielding as gravel, cut through the tense air. "Let her go."

"Or what? You think you can take on all of us? I know you're tough, but you're vastly outnumbered." The man gestured towards the group surrounding them, a dozen or so individuals, each armed and ready, while Salty sat immobile, unable to assist.

"What do you really want, Stone?"

Joe stepped closer to Ava and the mercenary who held her tightly. He reached out, his fingers brushing through Ava's hair, a gesture that made Grits' blood boil with anger and a fierce desire to confront him, regardless of the odds.

Grits took a deep breath and managed to steady his racing emotions. His mind ran through the stark reality. There was only one reason Stone had been waiting for him, and that was to silence all witnesses and eliminate any chance of being exposed.

Grits knew that he and Salty were living on borrowed time. Their minutes were numbered, and the threat was imminent. Despite the growing fear and dangerous circumstances, Grits, deep down, believed he would find a way to survive. His ultimate goal was clear. He had to rescue Ava from Stone's clutches before it was too late.

"If all you wanted was her, you'd have been gone by now. Why the grand show?"

Stone's laugh echoed, twisting Grits' gut.

His finger itched on the trigger, impulses battling logic. "You know me too well."

"We were once teammates."

"True. True."

"What will it take to let her go?"

Stone's voice was steady. "First, put down that rifle. Then, carefully, remove your other weapons and toss them away, far from you."

Grits hesitated. Dropping his gear meant surrendering his chance to fight. He'd been ambushed once before, and it had cost him three men, and today, the price felt even higher. His and Salty's lives hung in the balance. He hated that he'd dragged his friend into this mess, fearing this might be their last goodbye.

"I'll rescue you, Ava." Carefully, he laid down his rifle, ensuring it was out of reach. Next, he reached for the gun at his side, unholstering it with precision, and tossed it on the ground beside the rifle. He then bent down to remove the gun strapped to his ankle, setting it aside as well. With deliberate movements, he unsheathed the two knives tucked at his waist, laying them down with the other weapons. Having disarmed himself completely, he turned his gaze to Stone, his eyes burning with intense hatred.

"How sweet." Joe nodded towards Grits. In response, two men swiftly closed in on him, their movements coordinated and efficient. Despite his efforts to resist, they seized him firmly, their grip unyielding.

"Let her go." His voice was filled with urgency and defiance.

"Oh, I will." Stone smirked. "We've got what we came for."

CHAPTER TWENTY-SIX

Ava's heart thundered in her chest, her fury blazing as she struggled against the man gripping her waist with iron strength. She couldn't fathom how they had been ensnared. They had been following the path, and then, out of nowhere, the men had emerged.

Now, all three of them were trapped. Would they be executed here, or were they being taken to another location for their demise? Ava was determined to fight to the end.

Without warning, the man released her, shoving her forward so she crashed onto her hands and knees, the sharp brush tearing into her palms.

They'd got what they came for? It was baffling. They had targeted her, not Grits.

"You could've had me anytime. Why now?"

The man, whom she assumed was Joe Stone, shrugged nonchalantly. "Not my call."

Grits spat on the ground, a deliberate insult to Joe that made Ava catch her breath. Why was Grits provoking him? And why did they want Grits when she was the one who had discovered the message in the breach?

"Let's go, men." Stone's command was firm, and he

turned around sharply, leading the way back out of the dense woods, his steps brisk and purposeful with Grits in tow.

Salty immediately raced over to Ava and instinctively placed himself in front of her, assuming a protective stance despite being unarmed, his eyes scanning the surroundings for threats.

"Grits!" Ava couldn't believe they were not following to rescue Grits.

Salty turned back toward Ava, his voice low and cautious. "Quiet. Be lucky they didn't kill us both."

Ava's eyes widened with concern. "But Grits? Why aren't you trying to rescue Grits? Why are you just letting them take your friend?"

"Don't worry." Salty's voice reassured her, his tone firm but hopeful. "We'll figure it out and rescue him, no matter what it takes."

Ava, struggling to understand the situation, looked at the men sneaking ahead as they tried to devise a plan. "Well, then, let's follow them."

Salty shook his head quickly, his expression grim. "That would only get us killed."

"Then how are we supposed to find him?"

The former SEAL looked at her with a mixture of confusion and resolve, as if weighing an impossible decision. After a moment of silence, he nodded slowly. "We'll find a way. We always do."

The woods seemed to close in around them as Ava decided she'd do whatever it took to rescue the man she loved.

After what felt like an eternity of tense silence, Salty

suddenly spun around and sharply motioned for her to follow. "Hurry up. We've got a long journey ahead of us."

Ava's heart pounded like a drum in her chest, her mind racing with frantic thoughts. She had to find a way to locate and rescue Grits. "Where are we headed?" Her voice trembled with a mix of hope and fear.

"HIS" was Salty's response.

Immediately, Ava's thoughts jumped to Stone, the leaker who threatened their safety. Yet doubts gnawed at her. Could she really trust anyone at the agency? She trusted Devon and Jesse, yes, but what about the others? Grits had never spoken about them, and that silence deepened her suspicion.

"Can we trust them?" Her voice came out tentative, barely more than a whisper—small and uncertain, a stark contrast to her usual confidence. Recognizing her hesitation, she slowed her steps, took a deep breath to steady herself, and fought to summon her calm amid the rising storm of doubt and fear.

Salty nodded decisively. "Yes. Grits trusts them, so we trust them too."

At the truck, Salty motioned for her to hop into the passenger seat and fasten her seatbelt. With a quick click, she was strapped in as he slammed the gear into Drive. The truck roared to life, and they surged forward, crashing through a rugged trail winding through the woods. She held her breath, eyes fixed ahead, as he navigated the maze of gnarled trees and thick underbrush at breakneck speed.

Clinging to the "oh shit" handle, she shut her eyes

tight, replaying the moment she was captured. Her heart pounded fiercely, as fear and confusion swirled. She'd felt like it had been the end, yet she also wished she'd had more time with Grits.

Why had they taken Grits and left her behind? The question haunted her, loud and unanswerable.

"Why do you think they took him instead of me?"

Salty shook his head, eyes fixed on the treacherous trail ahead, voice steady but hollow. "I don't know, but we're going to find out."

She didn't understand how or why this was happening. They had no idea where Stone would take Grits or what he'd do to him once they got there. Her stomach twisted into a knot of dread and anxiety. Would they torture him? The very thought made her stomach churn and her palms sweat. She couldn't bear the image of Grits suffering.

Turning her mind to something she could control, she decided they'd need to find the source of the encrypted message. That was the only way to uncover who was truly after Grits and what their motives might be. It only made logical sense. But then, a lingering question persisted—why would they let her go? Why was she spared?

Maybe Stone, despite his fierce exterior and battle-hardened attitude, didn't harm women. That was her only hope and the only explanation that made sense. Otherwise, it was utterly baffling why they'd have let her walk free.

Or, perhaps, this entire situation had nothing to do with the encrypted message at all. Maybe there was something else entirely at play. Something she hadn't yet seen or understood.

There were too many questions swirling in her mind, and not enough clear answers. She clung to a fragile hope that the HIS organization was as formidable and reliable as Grits had claimed. She desperately needed that assurance now, more than ever.

Ava opened the glove box cautiously, her fingers trembling slightly as she hoped to find the sat phone that was supposed to be safely stashed inside. However, before she could do more than grasp the handle, Salty halted her with a firm, steadying hand.

"They took it with my weapons. They took everything." His grim voice was layered with frustration and anger. The fiery edge in his tone betrayed his disappointment and determination, both traits that would be crucial if they hoped to see this mission through.

Ava's gaze flicked around, sensing the urgency and the narrow window of opportunity slipping away. "We're losing time."

Salty finally glanced at her, his eyes catching her in the dim glow of the fading light as he slowed down near a real road—paved, smooth, and almost out of place in the wilderness. "It's okay. We'll be fine. Just try to relax."

Easier said than done. While Salty might have had years of experience to help him maintain composure, Ava was a jumble of nerves, her mind racing from one emotion to another—fear threatening to overtake her, anger bubbling beneath the surface, and a deep-rooted hatred for those who had taken everything from them, all swirling within seconds and making it hard to breathe.

Turning onto the winding, narrow road, Salty accelerated quickly, the engine growling as they sped through a dense woodland area. The darkness of the night cloaked the path, with no streetlights or ambient illumination to guide their way, leaving only the harsh glare of Salty's bright headlights to pierce the shadows ahead. The limited visibility heightened her anxiety, as she could only see as far as the intense beams illuminated, revealing twisted trees and uneven patches of asphalt that blurred past in a flash.

She shifted in her seat, turning her head slightly to the side, unable to watch the dangerous turns and sudden bends that lurked ahead. Her stomach clenched with fear, each sharp maneuver risking their safety further. The thought that any misstep could lead to disaster chilled her.

"Do you think the message had anything to do with what's happening now?"

Salty hesitated before answering, taking a moment as if weighing his words carefully. She wondered if he even knew the truth. "I don't know."

She looked at him, her eyes searching his face, then pressed on. "Why do you think they left us alive?" Her voice cracked slightly, betraying the lingering fear she still carried from that terrifying moment when she'd been in that man's grasp, feeling helpless and consumed by dread. The question hung in the air, heavy with unspoken worries and the haunting memory of the danger they'd just escaped.

"That's what truly baffles me. There was absolutely no logical reason for them to keep us alive, unless…." His voice trailed off, causing Ava to lift her eyebrows in curiosity.

"Unless what?"

Salty shrugged nonchalantly. "Nothing. Just thinking things through."

Ava's eyes narrowed, her mind racing with possibilities. "Do you think they kept us alive so we could rescue Grits?" Her voice was tinged with a mixture of hope and suspicion. Maybe Stone had some hidden streak of kindness embedded in him. Perhaps he genuinely didn't want to hurt his teammate any more than necessary. Or maybe, as a puppet, he was just following orders. But if that were the case, wouldn't he have been told to eliminate all witnesses?

Salty nodded thoughtfully. "It's possible."

Suddenly, Salty slammed on the brakes, and fear immediately gripped Ava as her seatbelt jerked her backward against the seat, digging into her shoulder. In front of them, a deer stood calmly in the middle of the road, a fawn close behind, seemingly unaware of the danger. Ava's heart pounded loudly in her chest, a racing drumbeat of anxiety and adrenaline. She had immediately felt that they'd been discovered once again, the danger closing in around them.

After the deer suddenly darted off the road, Salty quickly stepped on the gas pedal, pressing down firmly as the vehicle surged forward. Within moments, they had veered onto a nearby highway, the asphalt stretching out ahead of them. Since it was late in the evening, traffic was light, with only a few cars scattered here and there. They smoothly navigated through the sparse vehicles, all of them racing past the speed limit, eager to reach their destination as quickly as possible.

"You might want to take a little nap." Salty glanced over briefly. "It'll be a couple of hours before we get there."

Ava, sitting stiffly in the passenger seat, shook her head almost immediately. She couldn't sleep. Not with the adrenaline still coursing through her veins, mixed with a flicker of fear and a dull ache of anger. It was as if her mind was wired beyond her control.

"Yeah, I really can't."

Salty nodded. "All right, then. Let's review the message you mentioned, just to ensure we don't miss any important details. Start from the very beginning, okay?"

Ava took a deep breath, trying to steady herself. This was something she could focus on. "It all started when the bank called me to investigate their recent data breach. As I sifted through the unfamiliar code, I stumbled upon a message. It was definitely not regular code. It looked encrypted, but it felt different, almost like a hidden message buried within the data."

"What did you do?"

She explained everything that had happened before she'd met Grits—her phone calls to the FTC and the FBI. Then, she recounted what had occurred afterward until they finally arrived at Salty's cabin.

"So, all I know is that someone was trying to kill me. At least, that's how it seemed at the time."

Now, she wondered if she had simply imagined the whole ordeal and whether Grits was actually the intended target all along. How could that be? Where did she fit into this complicated puzzle? Once they discussed everything they knew—detective-like, laying out pieces of the puzzle—Ava felt the heavy tug of sleep pulling at her eyelids. Her eyelids fluttered with fatigue, but she fought it, stubbornly resisting. She knew she couldn't afford to sleep now, not when so many questions remained unanswered, and danger still lurked in the shadows.

Finally, she slept.

CHAPTER TWENTY-SEVEN

The warehouse was filled with a pungent mix of oil, dust, and the metallic scent of blood, creating an atmosphere at once suffocating and ominous. Every instinct within Grits screamed that it was too late to escape the dire situation he found himself in. He was forced to his knees, his hands tightly zip-tied behind his back, and a warm trickle of blood ran down his temple from a gash he couldn't see.

Behind him stood Joe Stone, someone he had once trusted, now revealed as the traitor within their ranks. Stone held a gun to his head, his expression twisted with malice and a cruel satisfaction. "You're not going to fight me, Grits," Stone sneered, his voice dripping with contempt. "Not unless you want your brains decorating the floor."

Grits felt a chill run down his spine, his body frozen in place. He knew that any sudden movement could result in his death. He had already been brutally beaten by Stone's associates, seemingly for no other reason than their own twisted amusement, leaving him battered and vulnerable.

"What now?" Grits grunted, struggling with the zip ties that had become a cruel vice around his wrists, biting into his skin.

"Now, we wait."

"For the puppet-master? Because we both know you aren't man enough to orchestrate this alone." Grits taunted the man, his voice dripping with defiance.

The words hung in the air for a split second before a sharp blow to his head sent a jolt of pain through him, leaving his skull throbbing and stars dancing in his vision. Despite the agony, he focused on controlling his breathing, calming his mind, and pushing the pain to the background.

All he could focus on was the relief that Ava and Salty were free. Stone had made a colossal blunder by letting them escape, and Grits was certain they would rally HIS to their cause. With a team in place, they'd come to his rescue swiftly. If only they could locate him.

"Why did you let her go? She's the one who discovered the message." The situation was a tangled web of confusion, as no one would reveal the truth. Instead, they pummeled him relentlessly.

With a swelling eye, a split lip, and likely a few fractured ribs, he realized this was merely the prelude to something far more ominous.

"She could have been your ticket to freedom. Instead, you chose me, the one nobody wants."

"Oh, but you're the entertaining kind of leverage."

"What's your next move? You know Devon's relentless pursuit will never end." Grits was convinced that Devon would track this man down no matter where he fled.

Stone sneered. "You mean Devon? I'm far more

cunning than he is, and you all failed to acknowledge it."

"Is this just about your ego needing a boost?"

Stone exhaled. "No. It's about blackmail."

The tension in the room was palpable. "All right, spill it. If I'm about to meet my maker, you might as well reveal why you're dragging me into this mess."

"He discovered I was seeing someone and started blackmailing me."

Grits let out a dismissive scoff. "That's all? Just because you were seeing someone, you're ready to throw me under the bus?"

"You don't get it. I'd lose my kids forever. My wife would take full custody and move away, keeping them from me."

"Then maybe you should've kept your dick in your pants."

Stone chuckled, a sound that grated on Grits' nerves. "You think you're any better? Bet you were dipping your dick into that hot thing the whole time you were supposed to be keeping her safe."

Grits retaliated, driving his head into Stone's stomach, eliciting a pained grunt. The gun wavered, and Grits saw his opportunity. But just as he was about to make his move, a nearby mercenary leveled his assault rifle at him.

Grits froze, tension crackling in the air.

"Sensitive about that, huh?"

"Leave her out of this."

"Oh, she's definitely in this. You're just the warmup."

Confusion clouded Grits' mind. "What the hell are you talking about?"

"He desires her too, but his obsession with you was

even greater. He's found someone else to take care of her."

Grit's heart sank at the realization that Ava was in peril and he was powerless to rescue her. "Why didn't you just take her when you captured me, then?"

Stone shrugged nonchalantly. "She wasn't my assigned target. You were."

It was the most absurd thing Grit had ever heard, but he figured the other mercenary would lose his temper if he didn't get paid for capturing his target.

"What is this mysterious figure planning to do with her?"

"He's going to kill her, just like he's going to kill you."

No. He'd figure something out. He had to if HIS didn't find him. And he had faith they'd do it. Just would it be in time?

"And who exactly is this mysterious 'he'?"

"You'll find out soon enough."

Grits weighed his escape options, realizing there were none. He could attempt to break free from the zip ties, but only if Stone hesitated long enough for him to pull his arms up and then jerk them down, bending at the elbows to strike his stomach. But then, the other mercenary would shoot him. So, he was screwed.

Before Grits could decipher that remark, a man in a sharp business suit strode into the warehouse with the confidence of someone who owned the place. For all Grits knew, he might.

Senator Bill Landry halted in front of him. Grits instantly recognized the man from the heart-wrenching moment he delivered the news of his son's death. It was one of the most agonizing notifications of his life.

"Grimes," the Senator commanded. "Look at me."

"So, you're the mastermind behind this."

The senator's smile was as cold as the accusation. "You seem to have taken quite a beating."

Grits remained silent, the weight of the truth heavy in the air. This man was the architect of the betrayal and the relentless attacks on his and Ava's lives.

"You understand what this is all about, don't you?"

Grits' heart sank as realization dawned. "Your son." Could it be that the man had blamed him all these years? Grits had carried his own guilt, haunted by the loss of his men under his command. But he had done nothing wrong. They had been ambushed, a cruel twist of fate in the chaos of war.

"My son would be alive if not for you." The senator's voice was a mix of accusation and sorrow, echoing in the tense room.

Grits remained steadfast, his expression unreadable. "Senator, you know I can't talk about the mission."

The senator leaned forward, his eyes burning with intensity. "Oh, but I've been read into it."

Despite the pressure, Grits refused to breach protocol, especially with mercenaries lurking nearby. "Doesn't matter."

The senator's voice cracked as he continued, "Not only did you send them into a fight they couldn't win, but you were the reason my son joined the SEALs in the first place. He idolized you."

Grits felt a pang of guilt as a new piece of information settled heavily in his heart. He tucked it away for later, knowing it would haunt him.

"I've been waiting all these years for you to find someone to love, just so I could take her away. But you didn't, did you?"

Grits' mind raced to Ava, the one he had let into his heart. He couldn't bear to lose her.

"Did guilt gnaw at you so deeply that you couldn't bring yourself to care for anyone? Oh, wait, you did find someone, didn't you?"

Grits felt a chill run down his spine. Where was this tirade heading?

"Don't worry. She'll be here soon enough. After Stone told me how you reacted when she was captured, I knew I'd found the perfect woman to take from you. Instead of killing her outright, you're going to watch her die."

A chilling dread enveloped him. Had Salty not taken her to HIS HQ, as he'd instructed, in case something happened to him? HIS would shield her. There was no way this could reach her. If he could, he'd have brought her forward already. They'd have captured them together. Something was amiss.

Grits chuckled. "You don't have her. Do you?"

"Oh, but I do."

Grits' humor vanished, and his heart plummeted. They couldn't have her. No, they couldn't.

The senator glanced at his watch, noting the time. "She should be arriving shortly." His voice was tinged with a mix of impatience and satisfaction. "Once she's here, I'll have the pleasure of witnessing you fail to keep her by your side. And after that, your life will come to an end."

Two shots rang out in quick succession. The mercenary holding the gun on Grits went down, and a shot, sharp and precise, grazed Stone's arm, causing his gun to skitter across the floor.

The Russian twins.

Grits reacted instinctively, ducking and rolling with the agility of a trained SEAL, breaking his restraints. Stone let out a roar of pain, clutching his shoulder, but Grits was already on him, crashing into Stone with relentless force before he could regain his footing. HIS had arrived, and there was no time to worry about the senator. He had to trust his team to deal with the man. This was personal.

Grits unleashed a fierce punch to Stone's jaw, each strike driven by a burning rage. They fought, all fists and elbows, each trying to overpower the other.

Yet, even amidst the chaos, his eyes darted around, vigilant for any lurking dangers.

Suddenly, she appeared. Ava stepped into the turmoil, heading straight for them. His instincts shouted "No," but his mind confirmed that HIS had indeed secured the area.

In a flash, Stone's focus wavered, and Grits seized the moment, delivering a thunderous punch that sent Stone reeling, momentarily dazed. As Stone struggled to regain his footing, Grits swiftly latched onto his legs, yanking him back to the ground. With a deft maneuver, he flipped Stone over, securing his arms behind his back as if preparing to cuff him. A zip tie was thrust into his hand, and with practiced ease, Grits bound Stone's hands. Rising triumphantly, he turned toward Ava, the air thick with the thrill of victory.

But then gunfire erupted once more, this time from a different direction, reverberating from the rafters.

A hidden shooter.

Grits' heart skipped a beat as he witnessed Ava stumble, clutch her side, and vanish behind a crate. The world seemed to freeze around him.

He couldn't recall how he reached her, only that one moment she was standing tall, and the next, she was crumpled and bleeding. He fell to his knees beside her, his hands already slick with crimson.

"No." He pulled her close. "No, no, no. Ava, stay with me."

Her eyes fluttered open, her breath coming in shallow gasps. "Told you not…to make choices for me."

"You're not dying. You hear me?" His voice was shattered, weighed down by the enormity of the moment. "You are not dying."

A weak smile tugged at her lips. "You're so bossy."

"I'm serious." He pressed his hands firmly against the wound, desperate to stop the bleeding. "You can't leave me now. Not when I've just realized I can't breathe without you."

Her fingers, weak and trembling, curled into his shirt. "Then don't let go."

"I won't." His forehead rested against hers, and a tear slipped from his face. "I won't. I love you, Ava. Do you hear me? I love you."

She exhaled slowly, her eyes fluttering shut.

Grits silently pleaded with every deity he'd never believed in, hoping fervently that he hadn't spoken those words too late.

CHAPTER TWENTY-EIGHT

Grits sat silently at Ava's hospital bedside, his hunched shoulders a testament to his exhaustion and worry. His head was bowed, elbows resting on his knees, hands buried in his face as if trying to shield himself from the crushing weight of the situation.

After the medical staff's repeated requests, he had finally washed away the blood splattered on his hands, the crimson rinsing down the drain and leaving only the faint stain of his memories. He hadn't changed his clothes since riding in the ambulance with Ava, the same clothing that bore her blood.

His presence had been unwavering. He had only left her side when she was taken into the operating room, pacing anxiously outside, clutching onto hope as if it were a lifeline.

Boss peeked into the room with a curious expression. "Is she awake yet?"

Grits shook his head, a hint of concern in his eyes.

The team leader stepped in, his voice carrying a mix of urgency and intrigue. "I thought you'd be interested to hear that while Ava was at HIS, she, Devon, and Salty tracked down the hacker responsible for the message, and he turned on the senator."

Grits nodded, a pang of sympathy for the senator tugging at his heart. It wasn't the senator's betrayal that moved him, but the image of a grieving father. The memory of his own fear when he thought he'd lost Ava was still fresh, and the pain was more intense than he had anticipated.

"What about the other shooter?" Grits' voice was filled with a mix of anger and determination. This was the man responsible for Ava's injury, and Grits was consumed by a desire for retribution. He wanted justice, and he wanted it now.

Boss let out a weary sigh, his expression a blend of resignation and relief. "The Russian took him out." His voice was steady but tinged with sorrow. "He didn't survive."

Grits absorbed this information slowly, his mind racing with conflicting emotions. On one hand, he was glad that the shooter was no longer a threat, but on the other, he couldn't shake the feeling of uncertainty. Was this the closure he needed, or was there more to uncover? The question lingered in the air, leaving Grits torn between satisfaction and doubt.

"And get this," the team leader continued, "Devon offered Salty a job."

Grits' eyes widened in surprise. "Wow. Did he accept it?"

Boss shrugged nonchalantly. "He said he'd think about it."

Grits chuckled, shaking his head. That was classic Salty. Whenever Grits suggested something, Salty would always say the same thing. "Was Devon considering him for computers or as a field agent?"

"He gave Salty the option."

Grits whistled, echoing with admiration. "Devon must've been blown away if he offered him that choice."

Boss nodded, his eyes gleaming with excitement. "He was incredible. The three of them were so engrossed in those computers, you could've driven a truck right through the building, and they wouldn't have batted an eye." He tilted his head to Ava with a proud smile. "But it was Ava who cracked the case, uncovering the lead to the hacker behind the message. You should be bursting with pride for her."

He was proud of her, despite the blunder at the warehouse. Even though he had believed it was safe, he couldn't really blame her.

"Do you want me to stay?"

Grits shook his head. "No, I'll be fine."

"How about some coffee or water?"

He smiled warmly. "No, I'm fine, but thanks."

Boss hesitated, his hand slipping into his front pants pockets as if guarding a secret.

Grits narrowed his eyes. "What aren't you telling me?"

The team leader grinned widely. "Devon also offered a consulting contract with Ava."

Stunned by the unexpected twist, he turned to his woman, his eyes wide with anticipation. "Did she accept?" His voice was barely above a whisper.

"She said she'd need to talk to you first."

A wave of relief washed over him, and he clung to it,

savoring the moment. This was their chance to collaborate, to see each other more frequently.

"She'll take it." She would be drawn to the challenge of working with the system she had dubbed "impenetrable." She would want him to be safe, and he knew she would seize the opportunity.

"I'll head out then. Keep us posted when she wakes up. The team has completely taken over the waiting room."

"How did things go with the Russian siblings and law enforcement?" He was still uncertain about their legal status. They had transitioned from covert operations with the FBI to working with them, a move that left him baffled. He and his sister were exceptional operatives, yet they had chosen to join HIS instead. It was mind-boggling.

"Sebastian had to do some slick talking." Sebastian, being their on-call attorney, was always busy with their cases. They needed to avoid getting entangled in local issues and focus on their international missions. Less red tape and paperwork would be a welcome change.

Grits nodded, unsure of what to say. The man had saved their lives, and he felt a deep sense of gratitude.

Boss turned towards the door, only to spin back around with a knowing smile. "You chose wisely."

Indeed, he had. It had taken years to finally open up and trust someone with his heart. Ava was his soulmate, and he was determined not to rush their journey together. But he knew, deep down, that they would eventually marry and have children. He could already envision their future.

"Thanks." A feeling of warmth spread through him.

Boss nodded, offering a reassuring smile before leaving the hospital room.

Grits turned his gaze to the love of his life, his heart full of hope and love. He took her hand, careful of the tubes connected to her. "Ava, honey. You're going to be okay, and we're going to have a long life together." He chuckled. "I can see you barefoot and pregnant, carrying our children. It'll be a sight I can't wait to see...."

* * * *

Ava surfaced slowly, like dragging herself up from the bottom of a deep, dark ocean. The world came back in fragments—beeping machines, the scent of antiseptic, something warm and steady wrapped around her fingers.

Her eyelids fluttered open.

Hospital.

Ceiling tiles.

A dull ache bloomed in her side.

And Grits was slouched in a chair beside her bed, his large frame looking almost breakable for once. His hand gripped hers like a lifeline, his thumb brushing slowly over her knuckles, like he hadn't stopped since she passed out.

He looked like hell. Stubble, shadows under his eyes, bloodstained shirt like he'd peeled off his tactical gear and never bothered with anything else.

She squeezed his hand weakly.

He jerked. Blinking. Disoriented. Until his eyes locked on hers.

"Ava." Her name came out hoarse. Like prayer. Like

regret. Like everything.

"So, you waited to make dramatic speeches when I was nearly unconscious and couldn't hear them."

His breath caught. "You heard that? Back at the warehouse?"

"Every word." Her voice cracked. "Even the part where you said you couldn't breathe without me."

He leaned in, pressing his forehead gently against hers, careful not to disturb the oxygen line.

"You scared the hell out of me."

"Ditto."

He pulled back just enough to meet her eyes. "You're okay. The bullet missed anything vital. You passed out from blood loss, but you're okay."

She gave him the tiniest smile. "What happened after I was shot?"

He explained everything he knew.

"And Stone and the Senator?"

"Captured." His jaw clenched. "And HIS is clean. Devon's already started rebuilding the infrastructure. You started a chain reaction that's going to take down a powerful man."

Ava closed her eyes, relief washing over her. It had all come together perfectly. They had finally traced the message back to the senator and unmasked the mastermind behind the chaos she and Grits had faced.

"I heard you were offered a contract." His voice held a hint of excitement.

With a smile, she opened her eyes. "Yeah, I wanted to talk to you about that."

He gently kissed the hand he held. "I think it's a

fantastic idea. It'll keep Devon on his toes."

Despite the pain, she couldn't help but laugh. "They also offered Salty a job."

"I heard."

She closed her eyes again, trying to find solace in the darkness.

"How's the pain?"

"Bearable." The word felt like a fragile shield against the discomfort.

"Hold on. There are a lot of people waiting for you to wake."

Her eyes snapped open at the unexpected revelation. "What do you mean?" Confusion clouded her thoughts. She had no family nearby. Could they have been summoned and traveled so quickly? It seemed improbable.

"Alpha team and the brothers who are in residence. They've been here the entire time." He chuckled. "I think the men are scaring the other visitors with their all-black gear and empty gun holsters. They look like a bunch of mercenaries."

"Oh." She could imagine what the others felt like. She'd been intimidated when she met the team at HIS HQ. They'd been a glorious sight, though, knowing they'd be there to rescue Grits.

Ava's eyes welled with tears. "I thought I'd lost you."

Grits leaned closer, brushing a kiss across her temple like it was the only way he knew to stay grounded.

"I'm right here," he said softly. "And I'm done running, Ava. From you. From this. I love you."

Her throat closed up.

"I love you, too," she whispered. "Even though you have bad timing for speeches."

He chuckled against her skin, and for the first time in days, the weight lifted.

This was the beginning of something real.

EPILOGUE

Six months later…

HIS headquarters hummed with a palpable sense of anticipation. The computer systems, now fortified and revamped, stood as a testament to Devon's meticulous restructuring after Stone's betrayal.

The drama reached its climax with a resolution that tied up all the loose ends. The senator and Stone found themselves staring down the barrel of serious charges, including treason, alongside a slew of other offenses. The gavel was set to deliver a sentence that would lock them away for a long, long time, ensuring they wouldn't taste freedom anytime soon. Yet, amid the chaos, a flicker of sympathy emerged for Stone, who had been dragged into this mess through blackmail. The cruel twist of fate meant that Stone would be denied the precious moments of watching his children grow up anyway.

Grits realized he owed Justin Franks an apology for suspecting him of betrayal, yet Justin was blissfully unaware of Grits' suspicions, so he'd keep it quiet. Meanwhile, the elusive Charlie team had vanished once more, drifting in and out like the wind, never truly integrating with Alpha or Bravo team.

The loss of Daylan had sent shockwaves through the teams. He was the one member of Charlie team they truly knew, thanks to his invaluable support with Pup's and his operations. It wasn't until he heroically took a bullet to save Ava that anyone truly appreciated him.

Salty had joined HIS as an agent on Bravo team, and Grits wouldn't have it any other way, even if it meant his team was one member heavy. Initially, there were discussions about placing Salty on Charlie team, but Grits firmly refused. The bond between him and Salty was unbreakable, and they were a dynamic duo that couldn't be separated.

Through it all, Grits and his team had rallied together, their bonds stronger than ever, having weathered the storm of deceit. They had embarked on a series of missions, each more daunting than the previous, pushing their limits and testing their resolve. Yet, a shadow loomed over their success. Grits couldn't shake the concern gnawing at him about Nemo, his sniper, who seemed to be grappling with an unseen struggle that eluded understanding.

The sniper held his position with precision, but off duty, he was a ghost. This distance troubled Grits, as it was disrupting the team's harmony when they weren't in action. The team didn't need to be glued together constantly, but during their rare moments of downtime, Nemo seemed to hover on the fringes or concoct reasons to skip the fun. Romeo, Pup, and Casper, all newlyweds, didn't have many chances to break free, and when they did, they counted on the whole team to join in. As the last two bachelors, Speedy and Nemo were expected to spearhead the antics and keep the spirit alive.

He couldn't tackle that issue now, so he shifted his focus to the exciting new addition to his team—a female helicopter pilot. Originally slated for Charlie team, she was unexpectedly reassigned to his team at the last minute. The prospect of having their own pilot ready for action thrilled him. Additionally, bringing a woman into the mix was expected to add a fresh dynamic to the team.

"Why the big smile?" Boss inquired as he neared.

Grits' grin widened. "We've got our very own helicopter pilot now."

"I hear she's got a ton of war experience."

Grits nodded. "She sure does."

"But there's still just one chopper."

Ah, there was the catch. Grits doubted the brothers would splurge on a second one just to keep the teams happy. Nope, they'd have to draw straws for each mission where a helicopter would be a game-changer.

"What's the scoop with the twins?" He was referring to the enigmatic Russian duo, not the Hamilton twins. Boss, ever perceptive, understood immediately.

Boss let out a weary sigh. "I reckon they're feeling the pangs of homesickness. But from what I've pieced together, they torched those bridges when they defected."

Grits couldn't help but wonder what secrets they had bartered for asylum and their government contract. It must have been monumental.

"Do you think they'll ever consider returning to being spooks?"

Boss shook his head, leaning casually against the

table. "Nah. I think they've found a new thrill in this side of the contracts."

After a few more minutes of chatting, Boss finally excused himself and left the room. A handful of team members lingered, casually milling about. It was rare for both teams to be together in the same space, so they often seized the opportunity to head off together for some fun.

Ava walked into the war room and stopped, arms crossed, as she watched Devon work. She wore dark jeans, boots, and a fitted HIS hoodie with Consultant–Cyber Division stitched on the sleeve.

She looked stunning in HIS attire, igniting in him the desire to whisk her away to his home and indulge in their passion. Instead, he chose to approach her from behind, adding an element of surprise to the moment.

"I can hear your brooding from across the floor."

Grits' arms wrapped around her waist from behind. "It's called thinking. Some of us do that when we're not hacking the Pentagon for fun."

She smirked. "Allegedly."

He pressed a kiss to the side of her neck. "You're trouble."

"You love it."

He pulled her tighter. "Damn right I do."

They stood like that for a while—quiet, steady. After everything they'd survived, silence no longer felt like tension. It felt like peace.

Ava turned in his arms and met his eyes. "We're not in hiding. No one's chasing us. No explosions for weeks. You bored yet?"

He chuckled. "Not even a little."

"Good. Because I've been thinking…."

His brow arched. "That's either really exciting or very dangerous."

"I want to build something permanent. Something real. A digital defense system that HIS can use across every op. Proactive, not reactive. One step ahead instead of always cleaning up after the mess."

He brushed her hair behind her ear. "You've already saved more lives than you know."

"I want to keep doing it—with you. As a partner. Not just on missions." Her voice softened. "In life."

Grits didn't hesitate. "I've been yours since the moment you opened your front door."

He kissed her—slow, deep, and unhurried. No more fear. No more walls.

Just them.

When they finally pulled apart, she rested her head against his chest. "So…do we tell the team we're officially cohabitating?"

Grits grinned. "Only if you're ready for the office betting pool to implode."

"I'm sure they'll manage."

He looked down at her, smile fading into something more serious. "You really okay, Ava?"

"I'm better than okay." She kissed his collarbone. "I'm home."

About the Author

SHEILA KELL writes about romantic men who leave women's hearts pounding with a happily ever after built on memorable, adrenaline-pumping stories. She is a four-time winner of the Readers' Favorite Book Award for romantic suspense and contemporary romance.

As a Southern girl who has left behind her days with the United States Air Force and as a University Vice President, she can usually be found in Central Florida with her family and cats. When she isn't writing, you can find Sheila with her nose in a good book, trying to leash train her cats, or wishing she had a genie to do her bidding.

Ways to connect:

https://www.sheilakellbooks.com
https://www.facebook.com/sheilakellbooks
https://www.goodreads.com/sheilakellbooks
https://www.bookbub.com/authors/sheila-kell
Sheila loves to hear directly from readers. Feel free to email her at sheila@sheilakell.com.

Don't miss out on new releases, exclusive excerpts, and giveaways! Join her newsletter: https://www.SheilaKell.com/subscribe

Join her Facebook Reader Group:
https://www.facebook.com/groups/sheilakellbooks

www.ingramcontent.com/pod-product-compliance
Lightning Source LLC
Chambersburg PA
CBHW011240200726
48288CB00018B/3404